Shyster Murders

By Bob Moats

Rev. 0324141105

Shyster Murders

For information and address:
Magic 1 Productions
P.O. Box 524, Fraser MI 48026-0524
Website: http://murdernovels.com
Cover by Bob Moats
Photo from Fotosearch.com

Other Jim Richards series books by Bob Moats

(In Series Order)
Classmate Murders
Vegas Showgirl Murders
Dominatrix Murders
Mistress Murders
Bridezilla Murders
Magic Murders
Strip Club Murders
Made-for-TV Murders
Mystery Cruise Murders
Talk Show Murders
Sin City Murders
Black Widow Murders
Vegas Vigilante Murders
Area 51 Murders
Mortuary Murders
Hypnotic Murders
Sunshine State Murders
Blue Suede Murders
Honky Tonk Murders
Dark Carnival Murders
Lipstick Murders
Pasta Murders
Talent Show Murders
Shyster Murders
Campground Murders
Network Murders
Reunion Murders
Big Apple Murders
Kennel Murders
Trick or Treat Murders
Santa Murders
Wiseguy Murders

For a preview or to purchase a book, go to
http://murdernovels.com

What people are saying about the Murder novels by Bob Moats

Mr. Moats, I just got your novel "Classmate Murders" and have to let you know, I read it in one evening. That is the first book I have ever done that with. That was the most enjoyable book I have ever read. I just started reading e-books, and reading again, after getting my wife a Kindle. This book was my 12th, and the best. I just got Las Vegas Showgirls to (read) tomorrow evening. ?. I look forward to reading many of your books in this series. I have been searching for an author and books that were fun, entertaining reads. Your books are just the ticket.

Regards, A new fan, Bill from South Carolina"

****

Hi Bob, I just had to write you... Last week I purchased a Nook Soft Touch e-reader. I was downloading free e-books and downloaded "Classmate Murders" from Barnes & Noble. I read it that night and enjoyed it so much that I went to search for the next one (as listed at end of the book). Read it and searched again. After reading the second one, I did a search from my e-reader for you and bought ALL of the books. So in the last week I have read all of the Jim Richards books. Finished the last one early this morning. I only read at night 10-6 when my neighbor is asleep. As I read the books I sometimes laughed and sometimes cried. I could relate to Jim as we are both in the 60s. I liked how "Jim" refers to previous murders in each book. That is great for anyone who has not read the books in order and also as fast as I did. Anyway, I just had to write and tell you how much I enjoyed the books.

Nancie S.

****

Another very nice comment submitted through my website from a person named Micki P.:

"I recently was given a kindle for my 60th birthday. The first book I downloaded was the Classmate Murders and have now read every one of the them. Today I started on the Fatal Rejection series. Thank-You for the wonderful ride with Jim and Penny and all the rest of the troop. I have laughed and giggled thru the stories, my poor family gave me the strangest looks! Now I really want a little Yorkie!! I will be looking out for more of Jim Richards and since you are my #1 Author, anything of yours I can find."

****

Received a feedback form reply on my website from a Cassy B. Here's what she said:

"Well, I just finished all 22 of your novels. I certainly hope you are hard at work at your laptop. I haven't run straight through a series since John D.

MacDonald's Travis McGee series. I thoroughly enjoy your characters, the plot twists and the humor in all your stories. Keep them coming!"

Thank you to Sally Berneathy who edited this book and is editing my other books. If you need an editor for your work go to http://sallyberneathy.com for more info.

Thank you for purchasing this book, I hope you enjoy it as much as I enjoyed writing them for my faithful readers. Please feel free to email me to tell me what you thought about my stories. I can be reached at murdernovels@mail.com thanks again!

Shyster Murders by Bob Moats

Chapter 1

Alphonse Grisler has been accused of being a shyster many times. Judges called him a shyster. Even his clients called him a shyster. He was the best shyster in Las Vegas, and it never bothered him to be called a shyster. He wore it proudly.

A shyster is someone who acts in a disreputable, unethical, or unscrupulous way, especially in the practice of law or politics. I wasn't fond of either lawyers or politicians. That's what I thought about Grisler as I sat in the courtroom. He was working a divorce case and I was there to provide testimony about the unfaithful wife. I really hated to admit I was working for Grisler.

About two months ago, business was slow at my firm. Richards Investigations and Security had its ups and downs, but that particular time was down. I wasn't fond of shadowing spouses, but it was money. Earl and Trapper were off on their own adventures, which left me to handle the mundane case. Grisler wasn't the one who came to me, it was the husband. I finally agreed to watch his wife and get anything about her extra-curricular activities. Being unfaithful.

I gathered enough facts to help, and I eventually found out Grisler was handling the case. That didn't make me happy. My last exposure to Grisler was during my talent show case, but it was during Trapper's case that I got to know Grisler way too well. He was defending Carlos Hernandez who was accused of murder and trying to frame Trapper's girlfriend, Sam. Now I was helping the weasel to get a divorce for his client. Of course, the wife was screwing around on her husband, so she deserved the divorce.

The problem was that Grisler made her look to be the most evil woman in the world. I had evidence that she was unfaithful. That was enough. Why make it worse? He skulked around the courtroom looking like the evil, ugly creature he was. I was daydreaming about how Earl would find damaging facts to put Grisler in jail when I heard my name being called. I jerked my head up to see the Bailiff standing over me.

"Mr. Richards, you are being called to testify," he said with a smile. I knew most of the cops and officers in the Vegas judicial system, including this guy.

"Thanks, Charlie. I was daydreaming about putting Grisler in jail," I said quietly so the courtroom couldn’t hear. He laughed quietly, and I stood.

I went up and did the swearing in. I hated the swearing in. It made people look untrustworthy, having to swear they wouldn’t lie or they'd face charges.

Grisler came forward and asked me about my participation in the case.

I spoke into the microphone attached to the witness stand. “I was asked by the husband to follow his wife and find out if she was being unfaithful. I did so and have the file to prove Mrs. Phail was unfaithful.” I stopped. I didn’t want to say more than I had to.

“Your qualifications are, Mr. Richards?”

I didn't enjoy having to explain my qualifications. Grisler knew them, and because of my notoriety around Vegas, just about everyone knew who I was. Hell, I saved Vegas once from a dirty bomb and once from a deadly virus. The press had canonized me numerous times, not that I was looking for praise, but it did seem ridiculous that I had to explain my qualifications.

“I have been in the private investigative service in Vegas for almost four years and have many famous cases I have been involved it. The Vegas

Vigilante case to name one. You need more?" I looked at the judge. He smiled then nodded. There was no jury, it was a divorce court case and none was needed.

"Mr. Richards, explain your procedure for tailing…pardon me…following Mrs. Phail."

I explained what I had done to tail the wife. I had my case file to fall back on.

I was on the stand for about twenty minutes as Grisler interrogated me. I thought he should save it for Mrs.Phail.

Finally he said, "No further questions." He went back to the table and sat.

The attorney for the wife said he had no questions. What could he do? Grisler made the wife look bad, and I had nothing her attorney would want, just more bad news.

I was excused and left the stand. Finally outside the courthouse, I took a breath and relaxed. I really hated lawyers and courts. They can twist the facts and lead the case into whatever way they want to go. I would avoid spousal cases like the plague in the future.

My firm had its share of spousal cases, and they all ended up being a mess. I was lucky that day that I didn't have to go through worse. Trapper and Earl both had their cases following wives and husbands. I remembered the time Trapper followed the crazy wife of the murdered victim during the hypnotic case. She ended up being our number one suspect in the murder. Later she proved to be just a nutcase and wasn't involved in the murders. But she provided us with hours of fun, I thought sarcastically.

"Mr. Richards, I need my husband followed," came a voice from behind me. My body tightened up, and I turned to refuse the case. It was Penny.

"You are just so funny," I said. "I'm not taking any more spousal cases so hire someone else to tail me. But be forewarned, I'm clever and stealthy, just ask Lacey." I was trying not to laugh, but it didn't work.

She kissed my cheek and said, "I was in the office and Lacey said you were here, so I thought I'd come over to give you moral support. I know you don't like lawyers."

"Don't like is too tame a phrase. I detest them. So what's happening in your world?"

"Good news, my show is going national again. The CW network wants me back and did their best to woo me. I'm going to make more money than I did the first time they hosted my show. Vegas is the big attraction, and I'm the big show in town, so they want me back."

"Well, that is good news. How's Gordy taking it?" I asked.

"Taking it? He's climbing the walls over it. He was doing his best to get this meeting with the network to push my show. He showed them clips from my past shows here and they loved it. Now they want to tape and run the shows from here like they did in Detroit. The time frame is the same as I did in Michigan. Taping the show early in the morning then broadcasting in the east around one p.m. and here around ten a.m."

"So you have to tape by eight a.m.?" I asked.

"Yep, just two hours earlier than I'm being broadcast now," she said with a big smile.

"That's great, we should celebrate. Have you eaten yet?" I asked.

"No, I finished for the day at the studio and went to your office after. I'm here and hungry now that you bring it up."

"Okay, shall we go to Angelo's restaurant where I will dine you in splendor?" I smiled.

"Splendor? How nice. Will there be violins?" she said.

"I'll see if Angelo can whip up some violins." I took her to her car and said to meet me at Angelo's.

I went to find my car and get away from the courthouse. I wandered around being a bit lost in the vast parking lot. I finally found my car but was intercepted by Grisler.

"What do you want, Grisler?" I asked, not happy to be stopped by him.

"I want to hire you," he said simply.

I wanted to tell him to go to hell, but something told me to find out more. "You want to hire me? Why?"

"Because you are good at what you do, and you do much better than chasing spouses. Let's forget this crap and I'll give you the case of your life."

He had my attention and curiosity. "Okay, what do you need, before I agree?"

"I need you to find out who murdered me."

He had my full attention.

*

Chapter 2

"Look Grisler, I have an important date with my wife to celebrate a great event for her. Can I come to your office tomorrow and talk about your unfortunate demise? When did you die?" I asked, knowing I was being flippant. The man seemed sincere about this. Maybe I should give him the benefit of the doubt.

"Yes, you can. But if I'm not there then you know I'm dead," he replied.

"Okay, I give, and you have ten minutes to tell me about your death." I stood firm and listened.

"I've been receiving death threats daily for about a week. I'm used to them. Everyone who loses a case to me hates me and sends their hate mail to me. But this particular death threat has been getting more violent. I need to be watched to avoid being killed. Can you manage this?"

"Simply put, no. I'm not in the body guarding business. Talk to my associate Buck Carson. He handles the bodyguards. Now if you were murdered, I would investigate to find the killer."

"But I'm not dead and I don't want to be," he said, looking more pathetic than usual.

I knew I could investigate the mail and maybe find the person or persons who wanted this evil little man dead. Even he didn't deserve to die.

"Okay, we can talk and I'll see what can be done. Tomorrow in your office. Now, lay low to prevent being killed tonight.

He didn't look happy but agreed. "I'll expect you tomorrow first thing," he said and walked off looking from side to side. Probably for the killer.

My cell phone buzzed. It was Penny. I answered knowing what she wanted.

"Where are you? I have a table already, and Angelo is trying to find violins," she said.

I laughed and said, "I'm sorry, I had an interruption. I'm finished now and will be there shortly." I hung up, got into my car and drove to the restaurant.

Angelo was by the door as I came in. "Mr. R, how nice to see you. Mrs. R is seated and not happy."

"Yeah, I was delayed. I'll take care of Mrs. R if you'll see if you can get a violin player." I grinned and went to the table.

"About time you got here. I was about to order," she grumbled.

"I had a brief conversation with the lawyer I was helping today. He caught me in the parking lot, and he had an interesting request."

"To defend you at our divorce?"

I tried not to laugh. "No, someone wants to murder him, and he wants me to find out who it is."

"I would think you would rejoice at a lawyer's death," she said.

"I would, but he looked so pathetic I felt sorry for him. Seriously, I can't let the man be murdered even if I don't like him. I'll go talk to him in the morning and see what I can do. If nothing else, I'll have Buck assign a bodyguard and charge him a fortune."

Our new daughter, Carol, came out of the kitchen and over to our table.

"Hey, Mom and Dad, good to see you," she said, flashing her great smile.

"Well, are you working too many hours to even get a visit in with us?" I asked.

"It seems so, but I feel so good here, I don't mind the extra hours. I really feel great creating dishes for the customers. Each plate is a work of art to me. I'm fixing a great meal for you two. I heard the good news about the national TV show, and I'm really happy for you."

"Well, surprise us," Penny said. "I'm sure anything you make will be delicious."

"I will. See you later," she said and went back to the kitchen.

We sat talking for about a half hour before we were surprised by the presence of a man with a violin. I laughed out loud then shut up. Angelo had found a violinist. I would have to really thank him for this.

Penny was swooning over the music he put forth. I hated violin music unless it was country. But as long as Penny was happy, so was I. The man was good. He was old and not a handsome man, but he could draw a bow across the instrument and make sweet music. Penny was wrapped up in the music so I apologized and said I had to visit the men's room. Penny waved me off, still focused on the musician.

Actually I lied. I didn't need the men's room. I just wanted to find Angelo and thank him. He was at the front counter talking to the cashier. He saw me and came over as I got close to him.

“Angelo, who did you have to whack to get a violinist?” I joked.

He grinned and said, “I got a friend who owns a Gypsy restaurant in town. She let me use him for the night.”

“Whatever it cost, you let me know. This is making Mrs. R’s night.”

“No charge, my friend owed me a favor for letting her skate on a bet. It was a small bet but she was thankful.”

“Either way, thanks again.” I shook his hand and went back to the table. Penny was still entranced by the music, and I sat quietly. She reached across the table and took my hand, then smiled at me. The man finished playing and I gave him a huge tip. He thanked me and went off.

“Perfect! A new career, fantastic music at our table, dining with my husband and a meal being prepared by our new daughter. What could be better?”

“Good sex,” I said with a grin.

“Don’t spoil the evening, sweetie,” she replied with a laugh.

Our food came along with Carol. She made sure everything was put out properly and we were happy. She went back to the kitchen and we ate our meal. It was fantastic.

"I'm still waiting to wake up from my sleep and find myself back in my bedroom in Michigan, and the last four years was all a dream."

"Well, don't wake up too soon. You have to protect Grisler first."

"Please pinch me so I can wake."

"Is Grisler so bad?" Penny asked.

"Remember 'Silence of the Lambs' movie? He needs one of those masks when he's in court. He's vicious when turned loose."

"Do you know that you spent the whole day without one call from Deacon or Lynn about a murder?"

"I was thinking that earlier. I was hoping not to be involved in any crimes for a few days. I'll go see what Grisler has and hopefully I can put Buck on him. Not that I wish him on Buck, but I don't need Grisler."

“Have you heard from the foxy chick lately?” Penny asked, resting her head in her hands on the table and leaning towards me.

“If you are referring to Detective Lorelei Paris, no. She went back to her precinct when Warren came back off medical leave. I haven’t heard a word from her. I’m hurt.”

“You’d better not be having secret conversations with her.”

“No, dear, we only text each other.”

Angelo came up and asked how everything was going.

“Angelo, by the end of this year you should be a wealthy man from this place,” I said as I looked around the room at all the full tables of people.

He laughed and said, “The place is booked with reservations through the end of the month and a lot beyond. My mother said she’d come out soon to see the place.”

“Angelo, I think that was a nice touch putting your family portrait up in the lobby,” Penny said.

“Gino didn’t even mind having his picture taken. I guess he’s mellowing for a mob boss. And he even gave his blessing to hang the portrait. Mom argued about it, but I won her over."

Angelo was called over by a waitress and he left us. I took the bill from our waitress and put my bank card on the tray. She took the tray and went off.

"Now what special thing would you like to do?" I asked. "It's still early."

"Can you get us into see the production of LOVE by Cirque du Soleil?"

"That's in the Mirage Hotel. I'll call a friend there and see if he has any comp tickets."

"You're bucking for a promotion, aren't you?"

"Something like that, or maybe something later tonight."

"Well, we'll see," she said, with her trademark evil smile.

*

Chapter 3

My friend came through with the tickets, and we drove to the Mirage Hotel. The fake volcano out front was erupting with colors, such a pretty sight. No wonder I loved the strip.

The show was excellent. We enjoyed it then left to go back home. It was late and our toy Yorkie, Willy, probably had the kitchen torn up by that time. I had to drive Penny back to the restaurant to get her car, then I waited for her to pull out and followed. I pulled into the drive after Penny put her car in the garage and pulled in, also.

Penny was already in the house and I was closing the garage door when I heard a loud noise. I ran in to find Alphonse Grisler on the kitchen floor. Penny was holding the fire extinguisher from the hallway in her hands.

"I hit him. It was the closest thing I could see, so I grabbed the extinguisher and hit him. Who is he?" she asked bending over the body. I hoped she didn't kill him before I could find out who wanted to kill him. I checked him. He was still alive, thankfully.

"He's Grisler. How the hell did he get in here?" I said looking around for Willy. I finally heard him barking out back at the patio door. I opened the door and he came flying in, stopping short of Grisler and yapping loudly. He had to be scolding him for being locked out.

"Why is he here? You were supposed to meet him in the morning," Penny said, on the verge of anger.

"Well, maybe we should wake him to see," I said as I got a glass of water and poured it on his head. I didn't know if that was standard procedure for waking an unconscious person, but it seemed to work in the movies. He stirred finally. I bent down to help him up. He sputtered something in a strange language.

"Richards, who hit me?" he said in a language I could understand.

"My wife. Why are you in my home?" I asked, shaking him gently to get him to wake up fully. I sat him on a chair at the dining room table. Penny was still clutching the extinguisher, I presume ready to use it again. I took it from her and put it on the table.

"Talk, Grisler. Why did you break into our home?" I said.

"I didn't break in. The patio door was unlocked. I opened it and that dog came flying out. I jumped in and closed him outside. I almost was bitten by him. I should sue for you having such a vicious animal," he said staring at the tiny creature on the floor baring his teeth at Grisler.

"You still haven't explained why you are in my home. Talk fast or I'll call the police!"

He looked up at me standing over him and said, "Someone tried to shoot me tonight. I had to go somewhere safe, and you were the first thing that came to my mind."

"Wonderful, so you came all the way out here to get me to protect you…wait, where is your car?"

"I walked," he said quietly.

"Walked? From where?" I asked.

"My house. I just live down the road from you."

Great, I thought. The one man I couldn't stand lived within walking distance. Hey, neighbor, would you like to walk down for a bar-b-que? "So you came here to endanger me and my wife?" I asked. "Thanks a lot."

"I made sure I wasn't followed. Richards, please help me, I'm so scared." He looked pathetic, more so than when I talked to him earlier. I pulled another chair over and sat.

“Okay, talk to me, explain everything that happened tonight,” I said.

He took a big breath. The man was dusty, probably from walking here. He had to have walked or crawled across the back of the property lines, which was still undeveloped and dirty. We were at the bottom of the mountain range so our backyard was hidden from prying eyes. Which I liked.

“I arrived home around 10 and parked my car out front. I was going to the front door to go in when I heard a gunshot and felt something go past my head. I knew it had to be a bullet. I ran for the side of the house while the shooter kept trying to hit me. I’m knowledgeable about guns and rifles, they aren’t as accurate as they make them out to be. I zig-zagged to avoid being hit. I was hiding in the brush behind my home but I had no weapon. I knew you lived not far and knew you and your wife both have weapons, so I snuck here.” He looked at Penny and said, “I’m sorry if I startled you.”

“I’m sorry I beaned you with the extinguisher,” Penny said.

“It’s good you are quick. I could have been the killer,” Grisler said.

“Okay, Grisler, the shooter knows where you live. We need to put you someplace safe. I’m calling my friends in LVMPD since this was a shooting. They can get CSI out to your home to check it out." I pulled my cell phone and called Lynn.

I looked at Penny as she said, "I knew you couldn't get through a day without calling Lynn and Deacon."

Lynn answered her phone at their house. I knew they would be home. "Lynn, I hate to bug you so late, but I have a problem."

Thirty minutes later, Lynn, Deacon and a couple uniforms were at our house talking to Grisler. He explained again, then Lynn had CSI search around Grisler's house. It was dark by that time but they would do their best. They had to process the scene quickly after the crime or evidence could be lost.

Lynn stood before Grisler and forced herself to say, "Alphonse, I'm not fond of you." She paused. "But it's my duty to protect you. I'll see that you have protection for a day or two, until we determine what is going on. Do you want to spend a night in the lock up or back in your home with a couple officers to watch you?"

"Oh, God, no. I don't want to go back to my house. But I don't want to spend a night in jail with all those criminals I'm sure hate lawyers. Don't you have another alternative?"

Lynn thought on the subject. “I have no alternative. I could see if we can put you up in a local motel for the night. How would that be?”

“Better than jail or back in my home,” Grisler said. “The shooter knows where I live. Damn, will I have to move now?”

I almost wanted to encourage him to move, but I held my tongue. Lynn turned to me and said, “Jim, you have a guesthouse that’s not being used. Am I correct?”

I cringed and couldn’t think of any excuse to refuse the use of the guesthouse. Crap, she screwed me. “Yes, I do. Gee, I should have thought about that. But that puts him close to his home. Maybe the shooter will figure he’s still in the neighborhood.”

“I’m sure the killer is long gone now. I’ll have a number of officers scouring the area. That should make sure he’s gone.” Lynn smiled at me knowing she got me.

“Okay, Grisler, you can stay in the guesthouse for the night. But only tonight. Then you’ll have to make other arrangements,” I said.

“Thank you, Richards, I appreciate it. I won’t be any trouble,” he said.

You already are, I thought. I took Lynn's arm and carefully pulled her into the kitchen. I was careful because she was still pregnant.

In the kitchen I said, "Thank you so much, Lynn. I can't stand that man and you put him in my guesthouse. I want a cop to stay with him to keep an eye on him."

She laughed and said, "All right, I'll put one man in with him, just for the night. Tomorrow we'll get to the bottom of this." She turned and went out of the kitchen.

After the cops all left, except one to guard Grisler, I took the shyster to the guesthouse and got him set up. Penny was bringing in clean sheets and blankets while giving me the evil eye. This was supposed to be her day, and Grisler ruined it. I'd have to get back at him for that.

*

Chapter 4

"I don't understand. They could have put him in jail to protect him," Penny said as she crawled into bed. "I think he deserves jail time, to show him what it means to be behind bars."

"My dear, most of the men in county lock up are there because of men like Grisler. Lousy lawyers. He is usually hired to defend his clients, but he doesn't always win. So he has a number of enemies in jail who'd like to meet him in the prison yard."

"I'd like to see him in with them, too. He's a greasy little worm, and he spoiled my night."

"Come on, you had a perfectly good day. You got your national show back, had a great dinner and a violin at the table. Okay, so Grisler showed up at the end of the day. Just ignore that."

She sat in bed giving me a harsh stare. I said, "Would you like a nightcap? Maybe a beer?"

"No, I'm going to sleep. You can go offer a nightcap to your buddy Grisler." She turned her back to me and plopped her head on her pillow.

Oh well, I thought. I crawled in and tried to sleep. I knew it wasn't going to be easy.

Early the next morning I staggered out to the kitchen and saw that Penny was not there. I worried that Grisler got her during the night and was torturing her in the guesthouse. I jumped when Penny came up behind me and said, "About time you got up."

"I didn't sleep very well. I kept dreaming about being in a courtroom alone with Grisler. He was the judge, jury and both lawyers. It was horrible."

The driveway alarm went off, and I went to stop it. I flipped on the monitor and saw it was Deacon. I told Penny and went to the front door, letting him in.

"You're here early, and where is Lynn?" I asked.

"She had some bad pains so I took her to the hospital. They're running some tests to make sure the baby is all right. She finally threw me out to find out what happened with Grisler. Is he still here?"

"I haven't the faintest idea. I just got up. Shall we go see how our star boarder is doing?" I looked at Penny. She just rolled her eyes and went towards the bedroom.

Deacon and I went out back past the Greek god pouring water into the Koi pond, out the back gate and to the guesthouse. We came up to the door as it opened. The cop inside was holding out his weapon but put it down when he saw it was us.

"Jumpy?" Deacon asked.

"This guy is about on the verge of being shot by me. He was bouncing around all night every time there was a noise. I didn't get any sleep and neither did he. He's your problem now," he said and walked past us quickly.

I was trying not to laugh. Deacon walked past me into the building. Grisler was hiding in the bathroom and screamed when we opened the door. He relaxed when he saw it was us.

"I'm so glad you're here. Did you catch the killer?" he said in a panic.

"There is no killer yet, you're still alive," I said.

"He's a killer since he took a shot at me," Grisler shot back.

"Alleged killer. You're a lawyer, you should know that," Deacon said.

"Technicalities. He's a killer and I want him caught."

"Let's get out of here and go back to your home to see what went on," Deacon said and went to the door. I followed.

"Wait, what if the killer is out there waiting for me to show my face?" he howled.

"If you don't follow us, I'll shoot you in here," Deacon snarled.

Grisler scowled, but came behind us as we left the building. He stayed close behind Deacon since the detective was bigger than the shyster.

We went out to Deacon's unmarked car and drove to Grisler's house following his directions. He was right about being close by. His house was far too close to mine. But I wasn't going to move.

Deacon pulled into the drive and got out. Grisler was hiding in the back seat as I got out. Deacon opened the back door and just about dragged Grisler out of the car.

"Look, Grisler, the shooter is not around the area. He, or she, is long gone," Deacon said.

"She? You think it could be a she?" Grisler asked, looking startled.

"It could be anyone. Even a child who may have a grudge against you. Maybe your paperboy?"

Grisler stood straight. "I don't have a paperboy. Now you're being rude."

"I can get even ruder if you don't start cooperating. Now explain all the details of what happened last night."

Grisler went into his lawyer mode, recounting the events of last night. He strutted around reenacting everything short of becoming the shooter. He was preaching to the jury about his ordeal and then summed it up with his thoughts as to who the shooter could be. He went through about ten different criminals who would all love to murder him. I was mentally adding my name to that list.

Deacon had to stop him. “Okay, Grisler, we get the idea. This is not a courtroom. I just wanted the facts so I could have something to go with.” He turned to me and said, “CSI couldn’t find anything, they even came back this morning to see if they could come up with some new evidence. They came up with nothing.”

“Where did the shots come from?” I asked.

“From the trajectory of the bullets in the side of the house, the shooter had to be over there,” he said and pointed in a direction across the road that was busy with tall brush. I went in that direction followed by Deacon. Grisler said he was going in his house to change his clothing.

Deacon and I scouted the area that CSI had already checked twice. I figured it was useless, but I wanted to see. I turned and faced the house. It was a good area to do a kill from. Cover was good, and the house was easy to see. I looked behind me out to the vast area of land that was undeveloped yet. I had hoped someone wouldn't put in a subdivision of tract houses, spoiling the view Penny and I had from our house.

"So this would be a perfect place to wait for Grisler and shoot him. CSI found nothing? Not even a cigarette butt?"

"Nope, the shooter was very careful and he even used a branch of leaves to erase his tracks."

"I'm thinking this was a professional hit. Someone wanted Grisler dead and hired a pro. I'm surprised he missed Grisler. Either he was not so good or Grisler moves fast," I said.

"I'm going with Grisler moving fast. I've seen him moving around a courtroom like he had the devil chasing him," Deacon said with a laugh.

As we were standing there we heard a gunshot from inside the house. "Crap!" Deacon yelled and we both drew our weapons and ran back to the house.

Deacon went through the door first as I followed. It was quiet in the house and then Deacon yelled, "Grisler, where are you?"

We heard a noise from a hallway and had our weapons ready. Grisler came around the corner holding an older model .38 Smith and Wesson. I wanted to shoot him and claim I thought he was the killer, but I didn't.

Deacon went to him and pulled the gun away. "What the hell happened?" he yelled in Grisler's face.

"I'm sorry. I was loading the gun I've had for years and it went off. I'm not a man who enjoys guns, but I had this one in case."

"In case of what? Attack from coyotes out here? I hope this gun is registered, or you will spend a night in jail. Do you understand?" Deacon's face went a little redder than usual.

"It's registered. At least I did that right," he said quietly.

I felt a little sorry for him at that moment. He looked so pitiful. Deacon emptied the gun and handed it back to Grisler, with a warning. "Don't load this again. We will protect you even if it hurts."

I figured it was going to hurt before it gets better.

*

Chapter 5

"Do you have any cases this week?" Deacon asked.

"Just one, the divorce case that Richards helped on," he replied.

"Not that I wanted to help on," I said.

"You did very well, Richards. I'm sure the judgment will be in favor of my client. The wife is toast."

I wanted to smack Grisler, but held back. Deacon went to the window and looked out.

"What are you looking for, Detective?" Grisler asked. "You don't think the shooter will come back?"

"Never can tell. Do you have to be in court today?"

"Yes, two o'clock today. Final determination by the judge. I'm sure it will be good for my client."

Deacon paused, then said, "I'm going to assign you one of our detectives to watch you in the courthouse, but after that you need to lay low until we can gather more information."

"Lay low? That sounds like you're going to put me out on my own," he whined.

By this time, I figured Deacon wanted to smack him, too.

"Mr. Grisler, we don't have enough men to watch you. Because of your efforts to release criminals, we are busy enough trying to arrest them again. So blame yourself. I'll see that you are protected." Deacon looked at me. I figured I knew what he had in mind. I'd call Buck to see if he had an extra bodyguard available. Preferably a big, mean, intimidating one, someone to make Grisler cringe.

"Okay, Grisler, go get ready for your big moment in court," Deacon said to the shyster.

He went off, and I went to the window, looking out at our cars. Deacon came over to me and said, "Do you think the shooter will try again?"

"It's a good bet. I'll get someone from Buck to watch him, but we have to put him somewhere he can't be found. Maybe your house?" I said with a smile.

"Lynn would shoot me…and you. We can put him in a motel, for now.

"Are you going to watch him at the courthouse?" I asked.

"I'll hang around. Care to join me?"

"It may be fun, sure. Shall we go outside and scout around?"

We went out and to the street. I looked up and down the road, then in the direction of my house. It couldn't be seen, thankfully. It was still cool in the pre-afternoon, but the weather was on the cloudy side that day. I hoped there wouldn't be any heavy rain. The flooding wouldn't be welcome.

"So, I hear Penny's show is going national again. I'm sure she's loving it," Deacon said.

"Yeah, she's ecstatic about it. Now I have to share her with everyone in the country again. But it's what she loves, so I encourage her. I miss the days back in Michigan when she used to bring strange things home from her show and scare me half to death. I don't think that will happen here. She has too many celebrities to work with now. No longer how to bake cookies. She agonized all night because she burned the cookies she was making the night before she had the bakers on her show. Honestly, they were hard as hockey pucks." I laughed at the memory.

"Let's go shake Grisler and get him to the court," Deacon said. He turned as I was going to call Buck about a bodyguard. Suddenly we were both knocked on our asses by the explosion of Grisler's house.

Deacon came up first, cursing aloud, just about every swear word ever conceived. I stood, and we both ran towards what was left of the now burning house. We had to stop due to the intense heat from the flames.

"Damn, damn, damn!!" Deacon said as he pulled out his phone to call the fire department. He reported the incident, and we waited. I went around the side of the house to the area where Grisler's bedroom would be. Deacon came up behind me, and we could see the back half of the bedroom was still standing. I went to the window and looked in.

"Grisler's on the floor. We need to get to him before the fire spreads to this area," I said.

"Don't break the window, it could cause a backdraft," Deacon warned.

Deacon looked around the front of the house and saw a garden hose. He grabbed it and pulled the hose to the window. He had me turn on the water and started hosing down the side of the building. Then he cracked a small hole in the window and stuck the hose in. He was trying to cover Grisler with water, hopefully to keep him from the fire which was now entering the bedroom.

While we worked on keeping Grisler wet, the fire department came screaming up the road. I ran out to meet them and told the fire captain what we had. He instructed his men to cover the bedroom and get the man out. Deacon moved away as the men were working to cut a hole in the side of the building while a water pumper was brought up to squelch the fire.

Grisler was finally pulled out, unconscious but alive. The EMS unit came up, and the med techs worked on him. They put him on a gurney and rushed him into the ambulance and off to a hospital. Deacon found out where they were taking him and called for a couple uniforms to meet Grisler there.

Deacon turned to me. "This is not good. Not good at all." He turned back to the house, now being covered in water. "I'll have forensics go over this disaster plank by burned plank. The killer must have spent the better part of last night plotting this and setting it up. Grisler must have triggered something to set it off." He went back to the road. I followed. "Unless it was set off by remote." He looked around trying to see anything that would give him a clue. I looked, also, but saw nothing.

"I guess we just have to wait to see how the explosion started. Maybe the killer is not in the area, so he wouldn't know if Grisler survived. Maybe we can put out a faked news report that he was killed. It may make the killer back off."

"It's a plan. All we have right now," I said.

Deacon's cell phone buzzed, he answered and listened. He hung up and looked pissed.

"What?" I asked.

"The killer knows Grisler didn't die in the explosion. The EMT unit was just run off the road going back into the city. That was one of the EMTs, George Marston. He knows me. He said everyone is okay, minor injuries, and he called for another unit to take Grisler. He also called for police backup, and the patrol cars in the area arrived. They're scouring the location for the attack car from the description George gave them. We need to step up our investigation."

Deacon checked with the fire captain and CSI who had arrived. He talked a bit then we went back to the car. Deacon was quiet on the ride back to the precinct. I was sure he was not happy. Neither was I. Grisler had asked me to protect him, now he was on his way to the hospital, and the killer was still loose. I didn't like Grisler, but now it was personal.

We arrived and went in to find Lynn sitting in her office.

"How did you get back here?" Deacon asked.

"I called Warren, he picked me up."

"How'd the tests go?"

"Good. I guess I just had indigestion. That's what the doctor thinks. Otherwise I'm fine, and the baby is fine. Now, how did this go wrong with Grisler?"

Deacon flinched. I was sure he wanted to handle this without Lynn's involvement. He explained everything from taking Grisler back to his house to the EMT being run off the road.

Lynn was quiet, then stood. "The doctor did say my blood pressure was way too high and wants me to rest. I'm taking my car and going home. Weber said it was fine with him. You are now in charge of this mess," she said and kissed Deacon on the cheek. "Have fun."

She went out and Deacon stood there with his mouth open, looking surprised.

"She hardly said a word about the mess. I hope she's alright."

I smiled and said, "I'm sure she trusts you to handle it. Now shall we go do a bull session and plan our attack?"

Chapter 6

Deacon and I sat in Lynn's office discussing the events of the last day. Grisler wasn't on our favorite list, but he needed protection. Deacon called to check at the hospital to be sure there were guards on his room. He relaxed a bit then leaned forward to talk.

"We need to grill Grisler to find out who wants him dead. We need a list to go on," he said.

"That list would include Lynn and me. I don't know about you," I said with a smile.

Deacon ignored me and continued, "When I called the hospital they said Grisler was alive but unconscious, hopefully to wake up sometime soon."

"You know if he dies, we wouldn't have to worry about him," I said.

Deacon ignored me again. "Hopefully our APB on the attack car will turn up something. It's hard to hide a bright blue 2010 Ford Escape with a huge dent in the side from running an EMT unit off the road. There can't be many of those."

"You really want to solve this case, just to show Lynn you can."

Deacon looked at me and said, "I'll solve it one way or another. Lynn has been feeling worse lately, and I think she's ready to pack it in until after the baby is born. This is my chance to show I can do the job."

"Are you bucking for a lieutenant's slot? That would mean you'd have to leave homicide and be relocated elsewhere."

"Yeah, I know. But the pay grade and the prestige would be nice." He sat back and grinned.

"Lieutenant Francis DeAngelo. It has a nice ring," I said with a grin.

Deacon leaned forward again and said quietly, "I'd be really grateful if you could help me on this."

"I'd be honored. Shall we go see if Grisler's awake yet? Or we can go talk to his people in his office."

"Let's try his office first. His employees would know who hated him the most."

I laughed and said, "Besides his own people? I'm sure they would have a few words to say about him. Let's ride. I'll drive if you don't mind."

We left Lynn's office and went to my car. I drove the Crown Vic, since I decided to let the van rest for a while. We arrived at Grisler's office. I'd never been there before. I'd always avoided it. We dealt mostly on the phone about the divorce case. I wanted as little contact with Grisler as possible.

We entered into the overly gaudy, over decorated office lobby. I could see Grisler's hand in the decorating. The receptionist smiled and asked us what we needed.

Deacon flashed his badge and said, "I'm Detective DeAngelo, and I need to talk to all the employees who work here. Alphonse Grisler has been sent to the hospital with serious injuries. He was involved in an explosion of his home. Can you gather everyone in a common room so I can talk to them?"

The girl looked totally shocked and stood. "Yes, please wait here and I'll get everyone together." She went through a door off the side of her desk and disappeared. Deacon was walking around the lobby studying the paintings on the walls. Mostly art deco. I was amazed that there weren't any dogs playing poker.

She came back a few minutes later and asked us to follow her. We went through the door and down a long hallway. She stopped at a double wood door and opened it. She went in followed by us. There were about five people in the room, all looking confused.

The receptionist spoke. "Everyone, this gentleman is a police detective, and he has some bad news.

Deacon cleared his throat and stood a moment. I knew he wasn't comfortable talking to groups; I was ready to prod him if needed.

"Ladies and gentlemen, I'm sorry to bring you news that Alphonse Grisler is in the hospital." There was a mumbling by the people, all shocked by the news. "He was injured in an explosion at his home early this morning. He's alive but hanging on. I need to ask you to help me to find out who would want to kill Grisler. If you know of any person or persons who may have a strong desire to do him in, please talk to me now."

Everyone sat quietly looking shocked. One woman stood and said, "I can help you with what you want to know."

"And you are?" Deacon asked.

"Mary Franz, Mr. Grisler's personal secretary. I'll be happy to help you out."

Deacon looked around to the rest of the people and said, "I'll talk to Mary first. If anyone else has any ideas who may want to harm Mr. Grisler, talk to me. Thank you."

He motioned to Mary to follow him and we went out of the room.

"Mary, can we go somewhere quiet and closed off?" he asked.

"Yes, we can use Mr. Grisler's office since he won't be needing it right now." We followed her to another double door with a plaque reading "Alphonse Grisler, Attorney at Law."

We entered, and she asked us to sit. She moved to Grisler's desk and sat behind it. I thought this was strange. Was she trying to fill in for him?

"I'm Mary Franz, Mr. Grisler's secretary. Now I'll talk about Mr. Grisler's enemies. He had many, and all wanted him dead."

"Why?" Deacon asked.

"Why not? Mr. Grisler was not a very well-liked person, even by most of those he represented. He had a way of annoying people. Even us."

"You don't think someone in his office would want to kill him?"

"Oh, goodness, no. We all depended on him for our pay checks. We may not have liked him but we wouldn't murder him. That would be counter-productive."

"I can appreciate that, but now I need to know who you suspect would go to the extreme of hiring a professional hit man to kill him."

"A professional hitman? That's extreme, yes. Most of Mr. Grisler's clients weren't wealthy enough to hire a hitman. I'm assuming that it would take a good deal of money to hire a hitman. Not that I would know."

"Well, yes, most hitmen do charge a good deal of money for their work. You think Grisler's clients couldn't afford to hire one?"

"They were all seedy people, not well off and mostly junkies, drug dealers, prostitutes, men looking to divorce their wives. Not many big money clients. I often told Mr. Grisler he should shoot for better clients. But he wanted to help the lower class of people."

"Noble of him. I didn't know he had a heart," Deacon said, but I didn't think he cared.

"Oh, yes! Mr. Grisler occasionally had a big heart and often did a case pro-bono."

"He actually worked for free?" Deacon was amazed.

"Yes, he would take many cases that he felt were charity. He was a man of the people. Helping the poor and those who needed a break."

Deacon looked at me and frowned. "Maybe I misjudged him."

"Maybe we all did," I said and then asked the woman, "Did he have any cases that he failed to get his client off? Maybe the client ended up with a lot of jail time."

"Oh, yes, many times. Mr. Grisler wasn't the best lawyer. He tried hard but failed many times. He was good at divorce cases, but his clients who were being tried for murder or serious crimes would often end up in jail. I can get a list of those people, the ones I think would want Mr. Grisler dead."

"That would be helpful, thank you," Deacon said as the woman stood and went out of the office. He looked at me and said, "So, do you think she may be able to help us?"

"Hell if I know. She seems awful ready to be helpful, but I think she has other reasons to be helpful. But that's just my opinion."

"I've found your opinions usually mean something. You don't think she may have an interest in dumping her boss? It wouldn't be the first time."

"She could be a suspect. A disgruntled employee who wants to do her boss in. She's being very helpful in giving us details on who may want to kill her boss. Maybe to get us off her trail. It's a theory. But as I said that's just my opinion."

She came back in with a couple sheets of paper. She handed them to Deacon and said, "Here's a list of all the people I think would kill Mr. Grisler."

Deacon looked over to me again and smiled.

*

Chapter 7

"Thank you, Mary," Deacon said. "Now, how did you feel about Mr. Grisler?"

She paused a bit too long, thinking. I figured she was developing excuses. She looked at me, then Deacon. "I was not fond of Mr. Grisler. Have you met the man?"

I wasn't going to touch that.

She continued, “He was a man with a good heart for the slime of the city, but he was mostly a mean, rotten little creep. He treated his employees like they were slaves. He had no respect for women. We were just subservient workers. Everyone here would like to see him dead, but, as I said, we needed him alive in order for us to survive. Job opportunities in Las Vegas are not good unless you can count cards. No, I wouldn’t kill him. I just think about it every day.”

“Honestly said, Mary,” Deacon said with a smile. “So I can write you off the suspect list?”

“I hope so. I wouldn’t murder him or hire someone to do it,” she replied.

Deacon stood. I figured he was finished with her. “Mary, I still need to talk to the other employees. Can you send them in one at a time, please?”

Mary stood and came around the desk. “Of course. I’ll get them.” She went out.

“What do you think?” Deacon, still standing, asked me.

“I think she’s being serious. But that’s just my opinion.”

"You have a lot of opinions but nothing to help solve the case. What do you think?"

I sat for a moment then said, "I don't think. Well…I mean I don't guess. We don't have enough yet. Talk to the others and see what they have to say and maybe we'll get a better picture of Grisler."

The door opened and in walked an older woman, maybe in her 70s. Deacon smiled and asked her to sit. She went for one of the client chairs and sat looking like a woman off the cake mix boxes.

"Hello. And you are?" Deacon asked.

"Martha Wallace. I'm a legal aide. I help Mr. Grisler with things he needs to know to conduct his cases."

"So you are his Google?" I asked.

She laughed and said, "I guess you could see it that way. I use Google a lot and other sources to gather information for him."

Deacon sat next to her and asked, "How did you feel about Mr. Grisler?"

She did the same pause that Mary did and then said, "He was a difficult man to work for, but I liked my job so I didn't rock the boat. He asked and I answered."

"Did you have any beef with him, enough to want to kill him?" Deacon asked quickly.

She looked stunned. "Oh my goodness, no! I liked Mr. Grisler despite his ornery ways. He was a sweetheart to me."

I figured that Grisler probably thought of this woman as a mother figure. I wondered if he actually had a mother or was hatched from a lizard egg.

Martha gave us no more information than Mary did, so Deacon excused her. He talked to the rest of Grisler's staff. They all hated him, but all denied they would have murdered him.

"I have no idea if any of these people would hire someone to kill Grisler. They all wanted him dead, but I believe them when they say they wouldn't do it. Or hire someone to do it. What do you think?" Deacon asked.

"I agree with you. I saw no one with a good motive to do the deed. I'm sure they all had alibis as to where they were during both hits on Grisler. But the nice thing about hiring someone to do the hit, you can be in a crowd and have a great alibi for the time of the murder," I said.

Deacon's phone buzzed. He answered, listened, then hung up.

He looked at me and said, "Looks like Grisler isn't the only shady lawyer in town someone wants to kill. Just had a murder of Don Wallis, a lawyer worse than Grisler. I'm needed elsewhere. Shall we go?"

We said our good-byes to Mary and went to my car. Deacon navigated to a small building near Fremont Street that sat amongst pawn shops and liquor stores. The office was just outside Deacon's jurisdiction, North Vegas cops would handle it. I pulled in and parked on the side. There were a number of patrol cars and the Coroner's van parked in front. We went to the uniform at the door who was taking names of the people who entered.

"What's the story?" Deacon asked of the officer.

"The office staff arrived, and Wallis' door was closed. No one liked to interrupt him in the morning; he wasn't very pleasant they said. Finally the phone calls were coming in and Wallis wasn't answering his intercom, so his secretary knocked on the door. He didn't answer. She figured he wasn't in, so she opened the door and found him dead in his chair. One shot to the head, clean kill. Had to be a pro."

"Thanks, Dean," Deacon said, and we went in.

The office was quiet like a morgue. I presumed the people seated in the waiting room looking dumbfounded were the staff. Deacon saw the lead Detective, Mike Rowe, and asked him what he thought. He explained the same as the officer at the door.

"The secretary called 911, and the first responders moved everyone to the lobby. I got here shortly after and, since it was a lawyer who was killed, I figured it had something to do with your case. So I called you to take a look."

"Thanks Mike. I've got Grisler guarded in the hospital from the explosion in his home. The first attempt on him was sniper fire. He lucked out on that one. No one else was working early here?"

"No, Wallis didn't like his people to get overtime so they had to come in and leave at the times he set. They were to arrive late this morning. That was his downfall."

"I suppose the security cameras weren't working?" Deacon said as he noticed the ever present cameras that spied just about everywhere in Vegas.

"You got it. They were shut off. I got electronic lab techs coming in to figure how they were disabled. CSI is going over the crime scene now. It was a hit and run, quick and clean. I don't think forensics will find much."

"Thanks, Mike. Keep me in the loop on this."

"I will. How's Lynn doing with the pregnancy?"

"Like living with a grumpy grisly. She's due in a couple weeks they say, but I'm sure she wants it to end sooner."

"Well, congrats on that, Dad."

"Thanks," Deacon said with a grin.

Joe Lang, county coroner, came out from the office of the deceased and saw us. He came over and said, "Deacon, what are doing in this part of town?"

"I was called. It's related to my case."

"You mean Grisler? Is he still alive?"

"Last I heard, he's still unconscious."

"I'm surprised he wasn't blown to bits in the explosion from what I heard."

"He was lucky."

Joe looked at me and said, "Hey, Jim, are you helping the big lug?"

"Actually, Grisler came to me first to protect him and find the person who was threatening him.

Things just got carried away when someone took a pot shot at him. Had to call the big lug in after that."

"I'm not a big lug, stop that," Deacon said dejectedly and walked away.

"I think we hurt his feelings," Joe said with a laugh. "Wallis was killed by a pro. One shot to the forehead from what I would guess was a good distance. The killer knew what he was doing. So the big lug has to find out who wanted Grisler killed and whether this one relates to his case. I feel sorry for him, what with the baby coming soon, and now this. Watch him closely so he doesn't run for it." Joe saluted me and left, following his men with the body bag on the gurney.

I looked around for Deacon and saw him standing in front of the building staring up at the Stratosphere Tower in the distance. I shivered every time I looked at the thing, remembering when I was hanging off the side waiting to drop. It was not something I would wish on anyone. Then I thought about Lacey and how she jumped off the tower and landed in a truck of mattresses. Some people weren't meant to die before their time, I guess.

I came up to my friend and said, "What's on the agenda for now?"

"We can go to LV Medical and see what Grisler is up to," he said with a smile.

I replied, "Or what he's down to. Shall we go?"

*

Chapter 8

We arrived at the hospital after stopping for a quick burger and fries at Hot'N'Now. Deacon had to badge a couple nurses to find Grisler's location. He was happy that they were being difficult about where the lawyer was. The uniform at Grisler's door knew Deacon and stood to greet him as we came up, then we all went into the room. Grisler had a private room and was lying in bed, not moving.

"How's our patient, Louis?" Deacon asked the officer.

"As you can see he's still out. The doctors say he may come out of it anytime but we may have to be patient."

"Can you people keep it down," came a voice from the bed. Grisler opened his eyes slowly and said, "What the hell happened?"

Deacon went around the side of the bed and asked, "What do you remember?"

"Remember what? A huge explosion and I'm suddenly in a hospital bed. Or am I dead?"

"No, you're alive. What caused the explosion, do you know?"

"You're the damn cop, you tell me. I was getting clothes from the closet when I was knocked on my ass."

A doctor came rushing in and over to the bedside. "Gentlemen, you'll have to back up," he said as he started to poke and probe Grisler. The shyster started complaining and tried to get out of bed. We had to restrain him.

"You may have been lucky you were in the closet surrounded by the clothes, Grisler," I said standing at the end of the bed. He just stared at me. "It protected you from the blast."

"Grisler, Don Wallis was murdered today, in his office. Now you need to be a little more cooperative," Deacon said from over the doctor's shoulder.

Grisler looked totally shocked. "Don? He was my friend. How did he die?"

"Shot in the head while he sat at his desk. It was a professional hit. Just like the explosion at your house. Someone big wants to kill a couple lawyers. You really need to help us," Deacon said.

"Detective, if I knew who wanted to kill me or anyone else, I'd be more than happy to cooperate. I value my life." Grisler howled when the doctor poked his ribs. "Hey, that hurt. I could sue you for pain."

"I could inject you with a very strong sedative that would take you out," the doctor said with a big smile.

Grisler turn to Deacon. "You heard him! He threatened to kill me!"

Deacon looked at me and said, "I didn't hear anything, did you?"

I smiled and said, "Nope, nothing. I heard nothing."

"You two are useless! I want a new cop watching me. And I don't need some hack P.I. tagging along," Grisler howled.

"I don't tag, do I?" I asked Deacon.

"Nope. Shall we go and leave Mr. Grisler alone?"

"Sounds good to me," I said and we walked towards the door.

"Hey, you got to protect me! You better not leave me alone or I'll sue you and the whole damn police department!" he screamed from the bed.

Deacon stopped and turned back. "Be nice then, and we'll protect you."

Grisler went silent, then looked up. "I don't want to die. Please protect me. I'm sorry."

"Grisler, we need to find out who wants to kill lawyers. We thought it was just you. Now with Wallis' murder we have to take different look at this. You rest and we'll talk. There's a cop on your door," Deacon said, pointing to the uniform, "and he will be watching you closely."

Grisler just grunted and we left the room. "That man is an ass," Deacon said to me as we went down the hall of the hospital toward the exit. We stopped just short of leaving the ward.

"And you wonder why I despise lawyers. They are asses in court and out of court. Grisler proves that. I'm sure Wallis was just as bad. Now who would want bad lawyers dead?" I said.

"Most clients, I'm sure. Maybe the opposing lawyers. Maybe even a judge or two who got fed up with their theatrics in court. There's a wide spectrum of people wanting bad lawyers dead."

“Spectrum? Are you still using that word book Lynn gave you?” I asked.

The big man grinned and said, “I’m just improving myself. I got a child coming and I want to be a good father. And if I hope to make Lieutenant, I need to be at my best.”

"Deacon, you're always at your best," I said.

"Thanks, but I know I'm rough around the edges. So what do we do now?"

"Well, Grisler said he was receiving death threats. We could check and see if we can track the threats to a source."

Deacon looked back to the room Grisler was in. The officer was back at the door and a doctor just came out. Deacon turned around and headed to the door. I followed.

"Change your mind, Deacon?" Louis said.

"Yeah, I have a couple more questions to ask him." We went into the room and found Grisler asleep again. Deacon went to him and gently shook him. "Grisler, wake up. I need to ask you some questions." Deacon shook him again. Grisler didn't respond.

I went to the bedside and checked Grisler's pulse. There was none. "Shit, he's not alive. Get a nurse or someone," I yelled to Louis. He burst out of the room and we stood looking helpless.

"That doctor who walked out, do you remember what he looked like?" I asked Deacon.

"Hell, they all look alike," he said just as a bunch of nurses and doctors came streaming in. We backed off.

"The monitor was shut down," one doctor yelled. He looked towards the nurse across the bed and said, "Didn't you see the thing was off at your station?"

"No doctor, we were busy with a patient who fell out of his wheelchair. But it was only a few moments."

"Crash cart now!" he yelled. "He hasn't been dead very long. We may still pull him back."

They spent the next five minutes working on him and finally we heard a cough come from the man. He stirred as the medical team did what they could to keep him alive. One nurse picked up a syringe from the floor next to the bed and showed it to the doctor.

He looked at it and said, "Get it to the lab to see what was in it." He turned to us. "I'd say someone tried to murder him again."

Deacon turned to Louis and said to go see if the security videos showed who left this room when we came up. Louis left, and Deacon turned back to Grisler. He had oxygen being pumped into a mask as the doctor examined him.

"By indications, he had a heart attack. It could have been brought on by the injection from the syringe. When we get the results, I'll let you know."

"Okay, I know you, doc. Any other personnel entering this room will have to have I.D. and one other person with them. No one alone, understand?" Deacon said to the man. "Makes it harder for a hit man to try killing him again."

"I'll leave instructions for my staff. You instruct your officers to be vigilant." He turned to the nurse and said to watch Grisler until he returned. He left the room as Deacon and I stood watching Grisler breathing lightly.

"He's just not going to die is he?" I said to Deacon.

"I think he's too ornery to die. This is getting serious now."

Louis came back in the room. "I was just down the hall checking with their security. They will run the videos back to the time you asked for. They'll make a copy so you can take it."

"Great, hopefully the killer slipped up and we can identify him." Deacon pulled his cell phone and called for another officer to help. He turned to Louis and said, "When the new guy shows up, one in the room and one at the door. You two check every I.D. and verify the person. No one person in the room, two doctors or two nurses at any time. The cop in the room will watch closely what they do and ask questions. If you get a hard time, you stop them and call for another doctor, understand?"

"Got it. No one will get near him again without us knowing the deal," Louis said.

Deacon went to the door as I followed. We were outside the room now and he said, "We need to talk to the late Don Wallis' people. It may not be my case, but it is linked."

*

Chapter 9

We got the video from security to give to the forensic people to work their magic and see if they could get an ID. Deacon left instructions for the new officer who came to guard Grisler, then we left.

Driving back to the office of the late Don Wallis we talked about what we could do once we got there.

"Wallis must have had some kind of threat against him. Maybe his people would know," Deacon said.

"I don't know this Wallis guy. Never heard of him. Of course I never heard of Grisler until he came in to try and get Hernandez off from your last case," I said.

"Most of these bottom feeding lawyers don't get much face time in the papers. The press doesn't want to glorify them. So they take cases, take money and go on their way. You don't see people like Grisler on a high profile trial. They are happy with the low life scum who push or pimp."

"Push or pimp. Nice name for a business. Shall we copyright it?" I said.

"No, thank you, I don't want my name associated with pushing or pimping." Deacon laughed as he pulled into the parking area again. He parked in the same spot, and we went around to the entrance. There were still a few officers and detectives interrogating the employees.

Detective Mike Rowe saw us coming and came over. "What are you two doing back here?"

"We went over to see Grisler at the hospital. Someone tried to kill him again, in his bed," Deacon said.

"In the hospital? That's bold. Did he die?"

"No, we got to him before he went into the light. He's still out of it, so we came back here to see if you got anything on this murder."

"So far everyone who worked for Wallis would have liked to see him dead. So they're all happy now. I'm getting no feelers from these people. Since I believe this was a professional hit, it goes further than the employees. I think someone higher up in this town has it in for shady lawyers."

"With Wallis' murder, I agree. Grisler had three hits on him, all pro-like even though they failed. This is no convict out for revenge," Deacon said.

"For sure. Only Wallis' secretary was aware that he was getting threats. But as she said, he got lots of threats."

"Just like Grisler," Deacon said. "These lawyers are regular magnets for murder threats. Maybe we should put a warning out to all the lawyers we hate that they may be in danger."

"True. I'll have someone get on that. It may be nothing or could help. Maybe Grisler and Wallis were the only two targeted," Rowe said.

"We'll find out if another one comes forward. Get that message out, and we'll see what shakes the trees. Maybe we can compare all of them and see if they have a common trait."

"I'll get right on it. I'm finished here anyway. I'll let you know if we get a hit."

"Thanks, Mike," Deacon said as the detective went off. Deacon turned to me and said, "I'll go through Mike's murder book on this later. I'm ready to call it a day."

"It's still early. Are you wearing down?" I said with a grin.

"I didn't sleep well last night. Lynn was awake most of the night from the medications she's taking. I'm surprised she's taking medicine with the baby coming, but the doctors told her it was safe. She needs to get rid of the infection she has. Poor woman is suffering."

"I hope all goes well. The baby is due soon, right?"

"Now it's two weeks they say. But the doctor said if Lynn doesn't get any better, it may be a good idea to induce labor. I'm not fond of that idea, but if it's needed I'll have to go along."

"Inducing labor isn't that dangerous. My daughter-in-law had to have it done with my granddaughter. She came out healthy and happy."

"Thanks, keep reminding me that it's safe."

"It's being done all over the country. Think about the early Native-American women who went out to the woods and had to give birth alone."

"That's not happening, and I don't even want to think of it. Let's change the subject." Deacon was turning green as his cell phone buzzed. He answered, listened and then hung up.

"We need to get back to the hospital. Grisler is awake and making a fuss. The nurses want to euthanize him," he said with a smile.

We drove back again. I was thinking we should get mileage pay for this. Deacon was silent on the trip back. I figured he had a lot on his mind. The baby was almost due and Lynn was ill. I could see when Lynn was feeling bad. Deacon expressed worry with his eyes. I spent a number of years since I first met Deacon and got to know his moods. He wasn't in a good mood today.

"What's going on in that head of yours?" I asked.

"Too many things. Nothing you need to worry about. I'm all right. It's just everything is happening so fast. I was happy when Lynn and I fell in love. It was new for me. I never had much experience dating or living with a woman. Lynn knew that and helped me through it. Now, with a baby coming I don't know if I can be a father."

"It's not difficult. I've been a father for a number of years, only one son, but it wasn't all that difficult. Sure, I worried when he went out on his own. I would be lying if I said I wasn't concerned for him. But I can't be there every day for him. He has to learn like I did when I left my parents."

"Sure, then you moved back in with your parents when you were sixty."

"You know why I did that. My mother needed me to help with my sick father. It was hard when people made jokes about me living with my parents. I could have survived on my own, but they needed me. So I put up with the jokes."

"You were such a good boy to help your parents back then," Deacon said with a snicker.

"Shut up," I said as we arrived back at the hospital.

Grisler was griping about everything from the nurses to his bedpan. They wouldn't let him get out of bed. One nurse confided in me they did that deliberately, to put him through the discomfort of using the bedpan. I enjoyed watching Grisler looking humbled but grumpy.

"About time you two got back here. I can't believe you left me here alone with these two idiot cops," he said, motioning to Louis and the other officer, John.

"These idiot cops helped save your life. We could have let you stay dead, but that isn't how we work. You were pulled back from your grave, Grisler. Now give a little credit where it's due. Or just shut up." Deacon leaned over the man and made a face. Not a happy face, either. Grisler shrank back and shut up.

"Good, now we need to ask you some questions. Who do you think would want to kill you and Wallis? And how many more lawyers are at risk?"

Grisler was quiet for a minute or two. We waited. He looked around the room, surveying his surroundings. He made a few pained faces, I imagine from the three attempts on his life that brought him to the hospital.

"I have made many enemies in my career. I've lost many a case and my clients went to prison because of my incompetence. I was young and rash, but I learned over the years to be a better lawyer."

"You learned how to be sneaky, you asshole," came a voice from the door. Deacon, the cops and I spun and pulled our weapons.

"Franson, what the hell do you want?" Grisler yelled from his bed. "Shoot this man, I order you."

Deacon kept his weapon trained on the man. He was about thirty-something, good looking and well dressed. I figured him to be a lawyer.

"Gentlemen, I'm not a criminal. I'm Jason Franson, attorney at law. Please lower your weapons," he requested.

Grisler yelled again, "Shoot him, he's dangerous!"

Deacon turned to Grisler. “Shut up, we’ll handle this.” He turned back to the man and said, “Now what do you want?”

*

Chapter 10

"I was concerned for my friend, Alphonse. I heard he was a victim of numerous attempts on his life. I see he has survived," said the man with a smooth tongue.

He went straight to the top of my list of lawyers I disliked. One step above Grisler. Now that was really disliking the man.

Grisler was mumbling something in a strange language, the same one he used when we pulled him out of the wreckage of his house. I looked at him. He saw me and stopped talking to himself.

Deacon went to the new lawyer and said, "Are you friends with Grisler?"

"I am. I came to see if he needed any help," he said with a smirk. I didn't like him even more now.

I moved forward and said, "What kind of help did you think you could give him?"

"Well, I wasn't sure. That's why I came," he replied.

"He came to see if I was dead so he could take over my productive law firm," Grisler yelled from the bed. We turned to listen to him. "You are a vampire, Franson. You suck the blood from everyone, including your clients. I don't doubt it was you set up my murder."

Deacon looked back at Franson. "Good point. I may need to talk to you at length."

"You can talk to me all you want, officer. I have nothing to hide."

"It's Detective. Now if you could visit me at our precinct, we can see about ruling you out. Or not."

"Be glad to, Detective. I keep track of all my activities, so I can provide an alibi for any time you bring up."

His smugness was thick. I disliked him even more than before. I really hoped he was the killer.

"Since it seems Alphonse doesn't need my help, I'll depart," he said with a curt bow of his head.

"You will be dearly departed when I get out of this place," Grisler yelled, nearly coming out of his bed.

Franson smiled again, showing his sharp, shark-like teeth. "I'll be in touch with you, Detective," he said with an even wider smile. He handed Deacon his card, turned and left the room.

"Are we in lawyer hell?" Deacon asked aloud. "Grisler, we need to start talking, now!"

Deacon pulled a chair over to the bed and sat. I went to the other side and sat on a chair by the window. I looked out and decided to move closer to the bed. A sharpshooter could be lurking outside.

"Now, you have been threatened frequently. Who do you think really wants you dead?" Deacon asked.

"To start with, that ass who just left here. He's hated me for years. We are rivals and have been jockeying for pole position for years."

"Maybe so, but did he hate Don Wallis? Enough to kill him?"

Grisler was silent for a moment, thinking. "No, I guess not. They were good friends."

"Franson was such a good friend of Wallis, but he came here to see you," I said.

Grisler looked at me. "Did you get dropped on your head when you were a kid? Wallis is dead. What could Franson do for him? I'm still alive. He came to see what he could do to finish me off."

"Okay let's forget Franson for now. Who else would have it in for you and Wallis?

Grisler went silent again. We waited.

"There was one judge who hated us, Wallis and me. Well, he had it out for another lawyer, Matt Holland, too. The three of us were in fear if we drew him as our judge. I would even try to get a change of venue, but he would deny it. Then he would make our lives miserable the rest of the trial. I'd look into him if I were you."

Deacon glanced at me, nodded and went back to Grisler. "We'll be sure to do that. What is this judge's name?"

"Chester Harper."

"Chester the molester?" Deacon said with a smile.

"That's him. He was named after that Hustler magazine cartoon sex offender and pedophile. But it fits. He's a pervert, also. Never caught, but accused numerous times. Now who's going to look into a judge's foibles?"

"As much as I hate getting involved with judges, I'll look into him. Anyone else?"

Again the silence. Then, "There are four good possibilities, all criminals. Ones that the three of us lawyers tried to get off. We didn't, and we were threatened by them."

Deacon handed Grisler his pocket notepad and said, "Write their names and locations, if you know where they are at present."

Grisler took the pad and started to write. He handed the pad back to Deacon who studied the names.

"I know one of these men," he said and looked at me. "Lynn and I busted him a few times. He got off two of the times. He had a good lawyer," he said with a snicker. "Then he had Mr. Grisler and went to prison for ten years. If he's still in the system, he could have hired someone to commit murder."

Deacon stood. "These names will give us a place to start." He turned to Louis, still standing by the door. "Louis, keep a sharp eye on Grisler. Maybe both of you could stay in the room," he said nodding to the other man. Deacon signaled to me to leave. We did. We didn't say much on the way out. Deacon was mulling over things in his head, I figured.

Outside the hospital we stopped at the entrance. He turned to me. "I think things will slow down now, what with three failed attempts on Grisler. My men will keep a close eye on him, so I really want to call it a day and start fresh in the morning."

"What if Grisler gets murdered in the middle of the night?" I asked.

"I'll apologize to his next of kin and close the case." He grinned.

"Your heart really isn't in this, is it?"

"I have a sworn duty to protect the innocent. But Grisler is hardly innocent, is he?"

"Okay, I need to go to my office to see what's going on there. So we'll start early?"

"Not too early. I probably won't get much sleep tonight if Lynn is still ailing. I'll call when I'm ready to roll."

We went back to my car, and I dropped Deacon off at his car. We said our good-byes and I left him. I drove over to my office and parked in the back. The cowbell was still announcing anyone sneaking in the back door. I waved to the security camera that Lacey was probably watching. I passed Trapper's office, he was out. Earl was out also and so was Buck. Fine place of business, no one was even in. Although that could be good. They should all be out working a case and making us money. Not that I worried about money. I had more than enough in the bank, and Penny was going to be rich with her new show. I had to share her again with the rest of the country.

I went into my office and found Willy sleeping on my chair. I ruffled him and he came up barking. "Hey, don't bark at me." I put him on the floor and sat. He walked around my feet sniffing. He probably could smell rat. Grisler.

I felt the presence of someone at my door. It was Penny.

"Sneaking in to avoid working?" she said with a smile and a kiss.

"I don't sneak. As I said, I'm stealthy. How was your show today?"

She sat in my client chair and relaxed. "We had the big wigs from the network in to watch how we do the show. They were happy and said they'd have their own people in to take over the operations for the national show. We start taping in a week. They are already starting a promotional campaign for the show. I had to endure their publicity people taking pictures of me and the set. They said they'd probably dress it up a little. I don't know how much more Vegas they could make it, other than a thousand more flashing lights."

"Well, you got to push Vegas, good for the city and the tourism. They are turning you into their spokeswoman."

My intercom buzzed. Lacey's voice came through, and she said. "Jim, if you are going to be working today, you have a visitor in the lobby." I said I'd be right up and stood.

I kissed Penny and said, "I hope it's not another person claiming to be my love child. Carol was enough." I smiled and went out.

*

Chapter 11

Penny was hot on my heels as I went through the doors to the lobby. Lacey was standing at the counter talking to a well-dressed man of about thirty. He had the smell of a lawyer. I was guessing he needed protection, too.

"Hello, I'm Jim Richards," I said. I realized Penny was right behind me. "This is my wife and TV's famous Penny Wickens. How may I help you?"

"Real nice to meet you, Mrs. Wickens." Penny was going to correct him, but I just told her to let it go. He continued, "I'm Matthew Holland. I'm an associate of Al Grisler. He mentioned that you were helping him on his threats he's been receiving."

"I am. When did you talk to Grisler?"

"Yesterday early. Before his house blew up. That had me worried. I have been receiving threats also. Can you help me, too?"

"No one has attempted to kill you yet?"

"Not that I'm aware of."

"Did you know the late Don Wallis?"

"Late? What do you mean?"

"He was murdered in his office. You didn't hear about this?"

"No, I just got back into town today. I was involved with a lawsuit on a dude ranch in Colorado. I talked to Al when he called me, and he didn't say anything about it. I didn't know about Don. This is tragic."

"Did Grisler call you after his house blew up? You mentioned that you knew."

"No, I called his office when he didn't answer his cell phone. His secretary told me he was in the hospital and what happened. Terrible."

"Okay, we can discuss this in my office. Follow me please." I turned. Penny shuffled around me and went behind the counter with Lacey. Holland followed me through the doors to my office. I picked up Willy and put him in the hall, closing the door. I pointed to my client chair and sat at my desk.

"I've been working with a detective of the LVMPD, and we were at the house when it blew up. Grisler was fortunate to come out alive. Now he said you also shared threats from four men. I don't have their names, so be patient while I call my friend at the police department and get the names."

I picked up my phone and speed dialed Deacon. I figured he was at home by now, but he should still have the names. He answered.

"Deacon, I have Matt Holland, Grisler's friend, in my office. He wants protection also. Do you have the names Grisler gave you so I can have him take a look?" I listened as he dug around for his notepad. He gave me the names and I wrote them on my desk notepad. "Thanks, I'll fill you in tomorrow morning."

I hung up and pushed the pad to Holland so he could read the names. He made a few small noises I took as distress. "I know all these men. They don't like me very much and have said so in no uncertain terms. Do you think one of them could be the person doing this?"

"We don't know yet. That's what we are going to investigate starting in the morning. Do you have a safe place to go tonight?" I wasn't going to offer him my guesthouse, for sure.

"I have to go back out to Colorado for my trial. I came back to get some work here finished. It can wait. I'll catch a flight back to Colorado as soon as possible. You don't think this person will follow me?"

"I can't say, but don't tell anyone where you are going. Instruct your staff to say nothing also. If you value your life, keep it secret."

"I'll do that. I'm still packed so I can just throw everything back in my car and return to the airport. Please keep me informed as to what you find out." He handed me his card, and I shook his hand.

"I'll do that. Have a safe trip back. Call me when you get there so I'll know you're safe." I handed him my card and he left.

I came back out to the lobby as Holland was leaving the building. “So is he in danger?” Penny asked.

“Could be. There’s always that chance. He could also be hit by a car, that’s fate.”

“Or murdered by an irate wife,” Penny said with a sneer.

“Is that a threat?”

“Take it as you see it. Can we go home now? I need rest.”

“You gather up Willy and I’ll see you back there. Lacey, are the others off on business?”

“Trapper is on a case of a missing diamond from a jewelry show at the Venetian. Earl is missing in action. Probably spending time with Paula. Buck is signing up a couple new businesses for guards. I’m ready to go home.”

“It’s early but you deserve the time off, so go. Tell Tracey she can go, too. Lock up the front and put out the sign saying we'll be back in the morning.”

Lacey didn’t wait for me to finish. She was already up in the front lobby telling Tracey to go. Penny picked up Willy and went out the back door. I waited till Lacey and Tracey had left then went out to my car. As I was going to get in, Trapper pulled up.

"So did you find your missing diamond?" I asked as he got out of his Jeep.

"Yep, it was an employee of the show. Tricked him into a confession. Everyone is happy, and I have a nice check for payment." He waved the check and then asked, "Is the place closed up?"

"Yeah, I sent everyone home. I'm on a case of murder threats on lawyers. One down, and one had three hits but all failed. He's an acquaintance of yours. Alphonse Grisler."

"The greasy mug that got Carlos off for trying to frame Sam for murder?"

"One of his better cases. Although Carlos did get arraigned for related crimes associated with the murder. I heard Grisler wasn't happy."

"And you're helping to keep him alive? You are a saint."

"It's my duty to protect and defend." I smiled.

"That's the police. You are supposed to solve crimes and make us rich."

"Rich is something we'll never see, but we do well enough. I have a date with Penny, so the office is yours." I saluted him and got in my car.

I drove back home thinking about Grisler. Not that I wanted to think about him but it was my case even if Deacon was in on it also. The police had this way of getting in the way. But it saved me from having to work hard. Deacon was a good cop. Not the best, but he tried and was lucky many times. We got along, and he depended on me to pull his butt out of the fire occasionally.

I pulled into the drive and parked in the garage. I went through the short hallway to the kitchen. It was quiet in the house. I saw the patio door was open in the dining room. I went to the ugly Greek god statue, fed the giant goldfish in the Koi pond and then out to the pool. Penny and Willy were splashing around having fun. It made me happy to see her enjoying herself. I sat on one of the plastic chairs to watch them.

I heard a noise at the gate to the side of the house by the guesthouse. I had my hand on my Glock under my jacket, waiting to see what came through the gate. It was my daughter, Carol.

She was carrying a towel and a small blanket. I presumed Penny called her to come for a swim. She came over to me and kissed my forehead.

“Hi, Dad,” she said with a big grin. “Mom invited me over for a swim. I couldn’t resist.”

“Not working tonight? Angelo let you take off?”

“Yeah, it’s my regular day off. Although I could work seven days a week and not get tired.”

Penny saw Carol and called to her. Carol dropped the beach robe she had on and dove into the pool. Willy came up the stone pool steps and over to me, so I picked him up even though he was wet. He stood on my lap and shook, getting me even wetter. That was all right. When Penny got out she’d plop down on me, too.

This was a good life. I hoped the lawyers wouldn’t screw it up.

*

Chapter 12

As I sat watching the women and dog frolicking in the pool, my cell phone buzzed. It was Deacon.

“What’s up, Papa?” I asked.

"I'm at the hospital," he said, sounding far away.

"Grisler?"

"No, Lynn. The doctors are debating whether to induce or not. Lynn's temperature is climbing, and she's in pain. I'm scared, Jim."

"You want me to come down?"

"No, I'll be all right. Just wanted you to know so you can plan for tomorrow. I'll fill Warren in on the case and he can go with you to question the criminals. I don't want you going by yourself."

I didn't know whether to be offended or touched by his concern. I knew I could handle it by myself, but it would be better to have police backup.

"Thanks, I'll call him in the morning to see what's up. You hang in with Lynn and take care of her. Call me if you need anything."

He thanked me and hung up. I sat there worrying whether Lynn and the baby would be all right. Penny came walking up. I hadn't seen her get out of the pool.

"Why the long face?" she asked and plopped down all wet on my lap.

"Lynn is back in the hospital. They may have to induce labor. Her condition is not good."

Penny didn't say anything. She looked down and then said, "I hope she's all right. And the baby. The doctors should take good care of her."

"I hope so. If you're done getting my lap wet, I think I'll go in and work on my book. I'm about finished."

"Which one is this?"

"The Area 51 Murders."

"Aliens. Good for a best seller."

"You know there were no aliens in that case, just killers and a deadly virus. We'll see if it does well." I stood, pushing her off my lap. She kissed me and dove back in the pool.

I went back in the house and into my home office. I sat at my computer and brought up the Word file of the book. All I could do was sit there and stare at the screen. I was concerned for my friends. About twenty minutes later, Penny came in my room, dressed.

"Are you just going to sit there? Shall we go hold Deacon's hand?"

I smiled, thinking the same thing. "You read my mind. Where's Carol?"

"I asked her to watch Willy and not to drown in the pool. Shake a leg. Do you know where they are?"

"Yeah, Deacon told me which hospital they were using. He should be there."

I stood and we went to Penny's car and left.

Deacon smiled as we entered the waiting room.

"Why are you in here and not with Lynn?" I asked.

"They chased me out until they know what they have to do. Lynn is in bad shape. I think they want me to not upset her."

Penny sat next to him and took his hand. "It'll be all right. She's tough, and I'm sure the baby will be, too."

I sat on his other side but didn't take his hand. A doctor came in and up to him. "Mr. DeAngelo, if you'll come with me, we are going to induce. You can watch the birth."

I felt my heart skip. Deacon jumped up, almost toppling over. He balanced himself and followed the doctor. He turned just before leaving the room.

"Thanks, guys. You're the best." Then he disappeared around the corner.

I looked at Penny, smiled and said, "I think we are about to become Aunt and Uncle."

We sat and then wandered around the waiting room for about an hour. A nurse came in and said, "Mr. DeAngelo said to tell you the baby is fine. She's healthy and normal and safe. After they clean her up you can see her." She smiled and left the room.

I turned to Penny. She had tears in her eyes. I kissed her and put my arms around her.

"This is a momentous occasion. Besides my new daughter, this is the first new member of our little family. Deacon and Lynn will need our support."

Trapper and Earl suddenly stormed into the room carrying balloons. "Starting the party without us?" Trapper asked.

Penny said, "How did you guys know?"

"Jim called me and I called Earl. We couldn't let Deacon be alone for this," he said and handed the balloons to me.

Penny smiled and whispered in my ear, "That was nice."

"So has the baby been delivered?" Earl asked. He looked like he was in his pajamas with his long coat over that.

"Are you in your PJs Earl?" I asked.

"I was in bed when Trapper called. I rushed out before I realized I hadn't changed. So what? Lots of people wander Wal-Marts in their PJs," he said with a grin.

"Nice ducks, Earl," Penny said looking at the prints on his pant legs.

"Hey, Paula bought these for me. I like them."

Deacon came into the room. We all cheered him. He stood looking happier than I'd ever seen him. "I didn't faint when they pulled the baby out. It was gross, but beautiful. I held my own," he said proudly.

"This all didn't take that long," Earl said.

"No, it was simple once they induced. They wanted to get it over since Lynn has a temperature over a hundred and two. They were surprised it went so well."

"Is she all right?" Penny asked.

“Well, she’s still feverish, but they said they could have her stable by morning.”

“Can we see the baby?” I asked.

“She’s in the room with all the other kids. They cleaned her up and she’s resting,” he said like a proud father. “We can go see her now.” He turned and went out. We followed.

Looking through the window at all the babies resting in their little beds, Deacon pointed out his girl.

“Have you named her yet?” Trapper asked.

He grinned and said, “Penelope Jamie Wilhelmina Earlene Georgina Angel Carter-DeAngelo. It wasn’t easy to convert all your names to something feminine. We threw in Angelo's name, too. We couldn't figure how to convert Buck, so we used his real name, George."

“Your daughter is going to hate you one day.” I laughed.

“We’ll call her Penny for short,” he said with a smile at my wife.

“Thank you, Deacon. Thank Lynn, too. I’m honored,” Penny said with a sniffle. “Can we visit her now?”

“I’ll ask the doctor,” he said and went off.

“She’s beautiful,” I said.

“Oh, come on, babies are ugly when they're born,” Earl said.

“Don’t say that to Deacon, if you value your life,” I said. Earl gave me a big grin.

We were standing ogling all the newborns when Deacon came back. “The doctor said Lynn’s half out of it, but we can say hi for a minute or two. Follow me.”

He led us to a room down the hall from the viewing room. We went in and around the blue curtain that was pulled around the bed. Lynn was deep in her pillow looking tired. We gathered around and she smiled. I tied the balloons to the end of the bed.

“Thanks for coming guys, I appreciate it.” She looked to Deacon and asked, “Is the baby all right?”

“Sleeping peacefully. Everyone just wanted to say hi, then we’ll go and let you sleep.” He leaned over and kissed her forehead.

"Your baby is beautiful," I said, then looked at Earl and whispered to shut up. He winked and smiled.

"Did you tell them her name?" Lynn asked Deacon. He smiled and said yes.

"We are honored to be included in your family," Penny said as she stood next to Lynn in bed and took her hand. "The baby is really beautiful. Looks like you."

"Poor baby. She's not going into law enforcement, if I have anything to say about it." Lynn laughed.

"How about becoming a showgirl?" I asked. Lynn gave me a look that said I should shut up. I did.

"Deacon's sister is the only showgirl in this family. The baby is going to be a doctor or a lawyer," Lynn said.

I looked at Deacon when she said lawyer. He shook his head to tell me not to say anything. I didn't.

"She'll be anything she wants, and we will support her," Deacon said. "Okay, everyone out. Lynn needs to rest." He led us out and we went back to the waiting room. He was quiet for a moment. We waited.

"Thanks for being here. It was important to me and Lynn. You are good friends."

*

Chapter 13

Everyone left the hospital by eleven. Deacon stayed with Lynn for the night. The hospital said that was fine, though I think he would have stayed no matter what they said, and they probably knew that. Penny and I drove home in silence. I was thinking about the baby. I'm sure Penny was also.

Carol greeted us at the door from the garage and was holding Willy.

"How did it go?" she asked.

"Beautifully. It's a girl. The baby is doing fine and so are the parents," Penny told her as she took the dog.

"I don't think Deacon is fine. He puts up a good front, but I'm sure he's a wreck inside," I said.

"He's got many more years to be a wreck. Then when little Penny starts to date, he'll totally fall apart," Penny said with a laugh.

"I pity the poor boy that dates her. Deacon carries a big gun and doesn't ask questions, he demands," I said.

"Little Penny?" Carol said.

Big Penny gave Carol the rundown on the baby's name.

They were laughing as I headed out of the kitchen and to my home office. I heard Carol yell that she was going. I yelled my good-bye back.

I pulled up my latest book and sat once again staring at my computer screen. I was trying to remember what happened next while Buck and I were saving Las Vegas from the terrorist bent on spreading the virus stolen from Area 51. I felt movement behind me as Penny came up and kissed my bald head.

"This was a good night," she said and sat on the side chair. "Too bad you didn't think to take your camera."

"Yeah, I spent $1,500 for that great camera and I hardly take it out of the case."

"But you just like the feel of owning it, don't you?"

"I guess so. I promise to take it with me when we go visit the baby again," I said. "Are you ready for bed?"

"Nope, I'm a bit worked up with all that happened tonight."

"I know a way that will tire you out," I said with a grin.

"Do your best, I'll wear you out first." She stood and left the room. I followed.

~~*~~

In his office Harold Skinner, attorney at law and a pretty good shyster, was going over his oration to the imaginary jury. He paused when he heard a noise outside his office door. It was after midnight and he was supposed to be alone in the building. He liked being alone when he practiced his summation that would sway the jury to his way.

He went on, droning his well-practiced lies, and then stopped as the noise came again. He went to the closed door and yelled through it, "If you are trying to rob the place, I have a gun."

It was his last mistake. He placed himself in the center of the door. Guided by his voice, the three gunshots found their mark and penetrated through the center of the door instantly killing Skinner.

He fell to the ground getting blood all over his script for the murder trial he would not finish.

~~*~~

It was a beautiful morning and while Penny made breakfast, she was humming some tune I didn't recognize. It sounded like either "Battle Hymn of the Republic" or some song by Taylor Swift. I couldn't keep up with music nowadays. If I listened to the radio more often I might get to know the new crop of singers and bands. But I never had much time to listen except in the car.

I stood at the opening to the kitchen by the snack counter as she put my toast on the counter. I was surprised she made it for me.

"Thank you. You seem to be in a good mood this morning," I said.

"I am. I was thinking about that beautiful innocent baby named after me."

"And all of us," I added. "I pity that child as she gets older and goes to school. I remember in elementary school one friend of mine refused to say his middle name when asked by the teacher. He whispered it to her. I never knew why until later in high school when I found out his middle name was Primo. He was named after an uncle in Italy. My friend never cared to have been named that. Penelope Jamie Wilhelmina Earlene Georgina Angel Carter-DeAngelo is a mouthful."

"A beautiful mouthful. Now I have to get to work. Don't forget to take your camera in case you see the baby. I plan on visiting Lynn after I tape my show, so I'll see you later."

She kissed me hard and long, then grabbed Willy and went out the door to her car. I ate my toast which was cold now but tasted good anyway. I dressed, gathered my things along with the camera case and went to the Crown Vic. I sat in the front seat, pulled out my cell phone, and called Greg Warren.

"Hey, Greg, I suppose Deacon filled you in on the events of last night?" I asked.

"He told me this morning when he came in. He's here now. Want to talk to him?"

I was surprised to hear he went to work. “Sure, switch me over.” Greg pushed buttons and I got Deacon. “What are you doing in the office right after your baby was born?”

“Lynn said I was hovering and told me to go to work. I know I’m a worry wart, but this is all so new to me. I just wanted to be sure everything was going smooth.”

“Lynn doesn’t like smooth. She like things rough and unpredictable. That’s what makes her a good cop. Are you waiting for me?”

“If you want to go question a few suspects.”

“I’ll be there shortly.” I hung up and drove out.

I went into Lynn’s office but Deacon wasn’t there. I was standing at the doorway when I saw him coming in from up front where Captain Weber’s office was. He at least was grinning.

“Weber was congratulating me on the baby. He told me to take a couple days off, but I told him what Lynn said. He agreed. Are you ready to beat a confession from someone?”

I was about to answer when Detective Williams called to Deacon. “What is it, Williams?” he asked.

"Got a new dead lawyer. Just got the call. You want to take it since it's linked to your case?"

I could see Deacon was turning green again. "Give me the details," he said reluctantly.

Williams handed him a sheet of paper and went off. Deacon studied the paper and looked at me. "This is getting serious. We've kept Grisler alive but we aren't saving any others. I guess this victim didn't get the notice about lawyers being in danger. Shall we go?"

I followed him to his car and we drove the short distance to the law offices of the now late Harold Skinner. There were the standard patrol cars and the coroner's van. I didn't see CSI yet. Deacon parked and we went to the door. The officer at the door took our names and logged us in. They were starting to keep track of who came and went at crime scenes. Helped later for questions on what happened and who was involved.

One uniform came over to us and said, "We got a 911 call about forty-five minutes ago. The office help was coming in and the vic's secretary noticed bullet holes in the vic's door. She didn't even open the door, just called for help and got everyone out of the building."

"Smart person. Where's CSI?" Deacon asked.

"They're running a little thin this morning. Lots of activities out there in Sin City. They said they'd be here when they get a team free. I'm having everyone stay out of the office. The vic is on the floor in a pool of blood. He's not going anywhere."

"Thanks." Deacon told me to hold back as he went in the office. I could see him through the open door checking the body. He stood, looked at the door and then came out. "Keep everyone out," he told the officer and took me outside where the staff was waiting.

"Who found the crime scene?" he called to the four people standing quietly by.

One woman came forward and said she had.

"Thanks for the quick thinking and keeping the crime scene intact. Who's the victim?"

"Harold Skinner," she replied.

"Can I ask a personal question?"

She agreed.

"Would you consider Harold to be a shyster lawyer?"

She hesitated, but then said, "He certainly fits that description."

Chapter 14

"Mr. Skinner was a good man. He was just exuberant in the way of handling his cases, and he succeeded more times than not. I don't understand who would want to kill him. It had to be a robbery," she said.

"Why, was something missing?" Deacon asked.

"Not that I saw. We left the building before the police came."

"I'm sorry, your name is?"

"Beth Redding. I am…was Mr. Skinner's personal secretary. He will be missed."

"The other employees feel the same way?"

"We all liked him. He would go out of his way to help us when we had personal problems. He may have been a shark in the court room, but he was good to us."

"Did he often work late during the night?"

"He would stay late when he had a summation to make. He practiced sometimes all night. But he kept the doors secure. Someone would have had to break in or had a key."

"We'll find out how the killer got in as soon as CSI arrives," Deacon said as he turned to see the big SUV pull up. CSI team leader, Mike Morrison, got out and came to us.

"Deacon, congrats about the baby. I heard this morning. Why are you here?"

"Lynn chased me out. I was getting in the way," he said with a smile. "The place is yours. We need the facts."

"You got it,' he said and yelled to his people to get to work.

We stood talking to the other employees, asking questions about Skinner. There wasn't much more to tell.

After about an hour of waiting around, Morrison came up and gave us some facts. "Okay, the door was jimmied, possibly a bump key. Hard to tell, but it was a break-in. The killer shot through the office door. I assume Skinner was standing behind it when he was shot. The height of the shots through the door match the penetration in Skinner. That's about as much as we have now. No prints, nothing to go on. This was a professional hit."

"Thanks, Mike," Deacon said. "If you get anything more, let me know."

"I will and congrats again." He went off, following his team to the SUV.

Deacon went back to the secretary and had her follow him into the building. I brought up the rear. Nobody asked me to follow, but I did it anyway. Deacon had the woman go to her desk and sit. He stood in front of the desk and said, "Now we need to talk."

He pulled over a chair and sat facing her. I stood behind him waiting to see what he was going to do.

"Beth, has Skinner ever received death threats and if so, how?"

She sat thinking then said, "Of course he got a few. Mostly emails but nothing really bad or threatening to kill him. Mostly hate mail telling Mr. Skinner that they held him responsible for their troubles. That they weren't happy and wanted him to know."

"Well, someone wasn't happy to the point of having him murdered. Any of the hate mail really stand out or repeated?"

She thought a moment then said, “Yes, there was one. He was persistent with his emails. We received about four from him. I didn’t think anything about it, and neither did Mr. Skinner. He told me to ignore them.”

“Can you give me the name of the person who sent the email?”

“I have a printout I can give you.” She opened a file, took out a paper and handed it to Deacon.

“Okay, did you get the notice from the police that there were death attempts on lawyers in Vegas? Two have died already and one is in the hospital.”

She looked shocked. “Oh my, no, I didn’t get any notice. When was it sent?”

“I’m not sure. I’ll have to check with the detective who was supposed to send them. Can you go to your email program and see if it may have been sent?”

She typed on her computer and studied the list of emails that had come in. She made a small gasping noise and said, “Oh my, yes, it’s here. I didn’t notice. It came in yesterday. I’m so sorry I didn’t see it. Mr. Skinner could still be alive if I had done my job.”

“Don’t beat yourself up over this. Skinner would probably be dead even if you had warned him.

This was a professional killer. He would have gotten to Skinner no matter if he was warned." Deacon stood and turned to me. "We don't have much more here. We need to talk to our suspect list." He turned back to Beth and said, "Please take the threatening email printouts and give them to the officer standing guard. I'll tell him to send them to forensics for exam."

We left after Deacon gave the instructions to the officer. We went to the car again.

We sat as I was waiting for Deacon to finish reading the printout Beth gave him. "There's not much I can get off this. I'm not a geek. You are. Can you make heads or tails from this?" He handed me the paper.

I read the thing and did what I could to figure out anything to give us a lead. But there was not much. The thing was unsigned so there was no name. It came from a gmail account, not much help there. The name "careercriminal98" wasn't the best email name to use. It would point to a troubled person or someone with a warped sense of humor. I figured the forensic computer people could do better than I could.

"Sorry, I can't help on this. Your people are better equipped to dig into this person. Call and give them the IP address and name and see what they can find." I pointed to the info on the paper, and he pulled out his phone.

We drove from the office to the first address of the suspects from a master sheet that Deacon had. We pulled up to a house on the west side of town in a suburb with buildings that had to be built in the '50s. I wondered if they were radioactive from the atomic testing back then. I'm sure they were safe, but it would be hard to tell without a Geiger counter.

We exited the car and stood surveying the property. The house was a square building, boxy and just like the rest of the houses on the block. The color was pastel green, like the others. It reminded me of military housing, which at one time it probably was.

Deacon said, "Let go." We went to the front door as it opened. A bedraggled, run-down woman stood looking out at us.

"If you're here to collect on Greasy's debt, he's not here," she said in a voice worn from too many cigarettes or booze.

"Police, ma'am. We're looking for Louie Fressard. Is he here?"

"Greasy is out at the moment. I don't expect him back too soon. Where were you people when he was threatened by the bookies? They wanted to break his arms, but he talked his way out of it. Greasy was always smart."

"Do you know if…Greasy…has an email account?" Deacon asked.

"He's got a computer in his bedroom. I don't know what crap he gets into. He could be watching porn for all I care."

"What are you to Greasy?"

"I'm his sister. He's lived here since our daddy died. This is the family home. We've owned it since this city was next to nothing and the gangsters ran everything."

"Did Greasy ever mention lawyers, ones he may have hated?" I asked.

"He hated all lawyers. They never did him much good when he was in court. They never cared for him."

"Any one lawyer in particular?" I asked.

"Should I be talking to you? Are you trying to get Greasy in trouble?" she asked.

"No, ma'am. We're trying to eliminate him as a suspect in a couple murders. If you could talk, we may not need to bother with your brother," Deacon said.

"Murder? Greasy doesn't kill people. He may rough them up but never kill them. In the past he's worked for a couple families in town as a collector of bad debts, but he never had to kill anyone."

I thought of Angelo. He never had to kill anyone either. It wasn't a good way to do business when it came to collecting money. A dead man can't pay off his debts.

*

Chapter 15

"Do you know where Greasy was this morning around 6 a.m.?"

"Yeah, the bum was passed out on the couch. He couldn't even make it to his room. He had friends over last night and they all got stinking drunk. I finally chased the last of them out around nine. Greasy came to about ten and I told him to get lost. He did. I had a friend coming over and I wanted to be alone."

"So he was here all night through this morning?" Deacon asked.

"Yeah, just what I said. Don't you listen?"

Deacon looked at me and said, "Let's leave this nice lady alone." He stood and we headed to the door.

"Are you going to arrest him?" she asked before we left.

"No, ma'am, you've given him an alibi. He didn't commit the murders."

"Oh, well, I lied. He wasn't here this morning, so go arrest him. Take him away from here, please."

"We'll think about it, thank you." Deacon moved away from the porch quickly. I followed.

We sat in the car and Deacon crossed off Greasy's name. Well, his real name. He read the next one and then started the car. "Shall we continue our relentless search for a mastermind criminal?"

"You know that these people didn't commit the murders unless they're some kind of hitman," I said.

"Yeah, but I need to see what they say. Maybe they'll slip on the facts and give me something to look into them further."

"Boy, you really are getting the hang of this investigating thing, aren't you?" I asked with a smile.

"Stow it. I'm a new father who was chased out of the hospital by a very hormonal mama bear. I would like to have spent time with my daughter."

"You'll have plenty of time to spend with your baby. It's just the first day. You'll have so many more."

"I guess so. I'm just totally emotional about this. You should have seen the birth. It was amazing. I tried not to pass out, but it was so beautiful," he said with a quaver in his voice.

"Want my handkerchief?" I tried not to laugh. It was precious.

"As I said, stow it." He put the car into gear and peeled out.

We drove for about a half hour in silence towards North Vegas. Traffic was miserable and Deacon's only conversation was curses towards the other drivers. He could be a real mean person when angered, which is why I tried to never anger him.

We pulled up to an apartment building and he parked. He sat quietly, then opened the door and got out. I exited the passenger side and followed him to the building. He seemed intent on going after this criminal. I was enjoying the show.

He entered the front door to the vestibule and stopped at the panel that had the names of the tenants. He ran his finger down the lists and stopped on one. He pushed the button next to the name and we waited. Finally a man's voice came out of a speaker asking who we were. I looked around the vestibule and saw a camera above us. The little red light was blinking and I assumed whoever answered the bell was watching us. I tapped Deacon and pointed to the camera.

He pulled his badge and held it up towards the camera, saying "Police, I need to see Wallace Gethering."

"Don't know him, now go away," the voice came back.

"The name plate says he lives here," Deacon replied.

"They need to change that."

As we stood there, the inner security door opened and a woman came out. I grabbed the door before it closed and we went in. Deacon headed towards the elevator, and we waited for it to arrive.

"I'm sorry if I got a little carried away with the whole baby thing. It's just so new," he finally said.

"No problem. I understand. It's a tough thing to get through. You watch while Lynn does all the work having the baby."

"Yeah, just like when we work crime. I watch while she does all the work."

"But you've said you like it that way."

"Yeah, I guess I do. But with the baby, it's different. We catch criminals and send them away. We have a baby and we have to take care of it for the rest of its life."

"Would you rather take care of criminals for the rest of their lives?" I asked.

"At least I wouldn't have to change diapers," he said with a grin.

The elevator door opened slowly and we got on. Deacon hit a button for the third floor. He got the number off the name plate. I figured the guy was already heading out of his apartment after seeing us enter the building, but I wasn't going to mention it to Deacon.

The elevator took forever, but we eventually arrived and exited the creaky, shaking box. Deacon went down a short hall to a room on the right and knocked. We waited, then the door opened, surprising me. There stood a woman in a bath robe on the short side showing very nice legs.

"May I help you, gentlemen?" she asked.

"I'm Detective DeAngelo, LVMPD. We're looking for Wallace Gethering. Is he in?"

"He left about an hour ago. Sorry you missed him."

"Well, is there another man in this apartment?"

"No, just little ole me," she said trying to sound southern.

"Do you also do men's voices? The person who answered the call box down in the lobby was a man."

Her smile dropped and she looked confused. "Uh…I don't know what you're talking about."

I looked past her and saw a face peeking around a wall in the hallway. I stepped forward. "Excuse me, but may I use your bathroom? I have to pee real bad." I was still moving forward as she was backing up.

"Uh…I don't know. You have to go real bad?" she stammered.

"Oh, yes, real bad. Which way is the bathroom?"

By this time Deacon had slipped by me and was heading down the hallway.

The girl turned and said, "Hey, you can't go there."

Deacon replied, "You said you were alone. I saw a man back there. I just want to be sure you're safe and not being held against your will." He continued to move as he pulled his service weapon. I had my hand on my Glock just in case.

Deacon came to the turn in the hallway and had his weapon right in the face of a man standing with his back to the wall.

"Hey, don't shoot, I'm not dangerous. Sarah isn't being held against her will. She's my girlfriend."

Deacon kept the gun right where he wanted it and said, "I presume you are Wallace Gethering?"

"Okay, okay…I am. What do you want?"

"I just wanted to talk, that's all. You're making this harder on yourself. It looks suspicious, like you're hiding something. You aren't hiding anything are you?"

"No, man, nothing. I'm on parole and I thought you were my P.O. and I didn't want to see him today."

"I'm sure you can tell I'm not your P.O. so cut the crap and move to the living room."

Gethering slid out and down the hall towards the front room. Deacon was behind him with his weapon still at his side. I moved behind the girl in case she decided to do something stupid. Never trust a woman at your back while you are rousting her boyfriend.

Deacon stopped and motioned to the girl to follow Gethering. She did. Deacon had them sit as he stood hovering over them. I guess he was trying to look menacing. Of course, as big as Deacon was, he always looked menacing.

"Now, I just need a few questions answered," he said sounding a bit nicer now. "Do you know a lawyer named Skinner?"

Gethering didn't even bat an eye and said, "No."

"How about Don Wallis?"

Again, “No.”

“Let’s try Alphonse Grisler.”

That got a reaction. “Yeah, he’s the creepy little rat of a lawyer who screwed me up and got me sent away for burglary. It wasn’t a big deal but he made it worse. He brought up my past crimes which had nothing to do with the robbery. The jury couldn’t help but hate me. I’d kill that animal if I had a chance.”

Deacon smiled and said, “Is that a confession?”

*

Chapter 16

“Confession? Confession to what? I didn’t do anything to anyone. What am I confessing about?” he stammered, sitting up straighter now.

“Well, two lawyers were murdered and Alphonse Grisler has had three attempts on his life. Luckily, he’s too dumb to be killed. You just threatened him with murder. I’d say that’s a confession.”

"Oh, man! I may talk big but I wouldn't actually murder anyone. Least of all Grisler. He's working on my appeal."

"So you haven't started your sentence. Why are you on parole?" Deacon asked.

"I was sentenced for another crime. Stealing a car, two years ago. I got out due to overcrowding. I don't want to go back. I needed money so I broke into a party store after it closed. I got caught by the security people."

I wondered if it was Buck's guards.

Gethering stopped talking and looked like he might lawyer up.

"Mr. Gethering, I could take you in for further questioning or you could just tell me if you murdered the lawyers. Save me and the city time and expense."

"You're being funny, aren't you? I murdered no one. Get that straight. I'll take a lie detector test if you want."

"Not necessary. I'll be looking at you again, so hang around the city." Deacon turned and signaled to leave.

"Hey, I didn't kill anyone," he yelled at us as we left.

Out in the car, Deacon said, "I'll have to have Warren check the financials on all these people. We're not going to get anyone to admit to the killings. This is going to be a waste of time. If anyone hired a hitman it will cost a bunch of money. So I'm not going to chase any more. I need to get back to the hospital and see my baby. The little one and the big one." He smiled and started the car.

Deacon dropped me at my car and drove off. I thought about going to see Grisler and talk to him. I got into my car and went to the hospital. I went up to the floor he was on and saw the cop on duty standing in the doorway looking in. I came up and he turned to me.

"Hey, Mr. Richards, where's Deacon?" Louis asked.

"He's going to arrest his baby for being born," I said with a smile.

The cop laughed and I asked, "What's going on?"

"Oh, one of Grisler's clients needed to talk to him. He said it was okay to let her in."

I was a little concerned about that and went to the door to look in. Grisler was still in bed and there was a rather attractive woman seated next to the bed, listening as Grisler talked. She was dressed rather nice with ample cleavage showing in the silk blouse she wore. Her skirt was short and showed very nice, well-toned legs. She had auburn-red hair; Trapper would enjoy this if he were here.

I moved into the room and got a closer look at her. She had to be in her middle to late thirties, and she had a number of tiny freckles on her face. It made her look cute. She looked at me with attractive chestnut colored eyes that had a sparkle in them.

"Richards, good you are here. Come meet a client of mine, Peaches LaFarge," he said with a grin. "She may need your help."

I extended my hand and she took it. Her hand was soft and warm. I had to stop what I was thinking. Penny would know. "Nice to meet you, Miss LaFarge," I said, assuming she was single by the lack of a ring on her marriage finger. Although she had lots of jewelry on, she lacked a wedding ring. Actually, now that I was closer, she was quite gaudy in her attire.

"Thank you, Mr. Richards. Mr. Grisler was telling me about how you are a great detective," she said with a mouth full of very straight teeth, all bright and glowing. She must use one of those teeth whiteners.

"Well, I appreciate Mr. Grisler's confidence in me. I try my best. What is your problem that you need a private eye?"

"I was accused of murdering my boyfriend. I didn't really. He died a horrible death. His radio fell into his bathtub and he was electrocuted. His wife says I did it."

That took me by surprise. "His wife accused you of murdering her husband, your boyfriend?" I asked.

"They're separated, she's filing for divorce and he was counter-suing. It was all so messy."

"Who was this late boyfriend?"

"Robert Dillon-Zimmerman, the record mogul. He had a number of singers that he represented. Many were sort of famous." She smiled and then the smile went south. "I loved my Bobby. He treated me well."

"Zimmerman? Of Repo Records?"

"Yes, that one."

"I thought he was in his eighties."

"Bobby was older than I, but we loved each other very much. He hated his wife. She was such a witch."

I was getting a picture now of this whole affair. And I say affair. Typical Hollywood script. Young gorgeous red-head and the octogenarian involved in a torrid romance started by the hot young femme fatale for the old man's money and power. Geez, how many times have I seen this plot? The wife did it, of course.

I said, "And you need someone to solve the murder. But could it have been an accident? What did the police say and have they questioned you?"

"They're questioning the wife for now. I haven't been called yet. I came to Alphonse as soon as I heard she accused me."

I looked at Grisler. "You know the police will be investigating this. Why would you need me?"

"I don't trust the police. Peaches is a stripper at the Golden Shoe, and of course they are going to blame her for this."

Peaches sat up and said huffily, "I'm not a stripper. I'm an exotic dancer."

Yeah, and I'm James Bond, I thought. "Well, that could happen. I'll talk to my friends on the force and see what's happening on this." I paused and then said, "If my firm takes this case, who's going to pay the fee?" I wasn't being crass, but it was a case and I wasn't going to do it free for Grisler.

Grisler smiled and said, "I'll take care of it."

"Fine, just don't get murdered before you pay. We'll need a retainer."

"No problem. Call my secretary, Mary, and she'll take care of it."

"I haven't said we'd do it yet, but I'll call my friends and see if there's a case here." I was thinking of turning Trapper loose on this. He liked strippers and red-heads. This was perfect for him.

Peaches thanked me and stood. "I need to go to work, but I'll call you when I can," she said to Grisler. "Mr. Richards, it's so good to know you are on the job."

"Well, Peaches, if my firm takes the case, you'll be contacted by my associate Will Trapper. He'll take your case, if needed. I'm trying to keep Mr. Grisler alive for now and that will be taking much of my time."

"Whoever calls, I'll be hopeful." She shook my hand again and kissed Grisler on the forehead. He beamed and said his good-byes. She left the room and disappeared while Louis watched her walk away. He had a big grin.

"Okay, Alphonse, we need to talk." I pulled up the chair and sat. It was still warm from Peaches' nice rear end.

"She's quite a woman, isn't she?" Grisler said.

"Who? Peaches? Uh…yes, she's quite a woman. How do you know her?"

"I've represented her a few times for soliciting. But the prosecution couldn't prove anything. Cut and dried cases."

"So was she soliciting?"

"Richards, you know client-lawyer privilege. She's a nice girl but a little dense. Which is why she gets herself into these situations. She met Zimmerman at the club while she danced. He wasn't interested in sex, just having her on his arm."

"Eye candy, eh? He wanted to look good for all his friends and business associates."

"Yep, Zimmerman couldn't get it up if he tried a whole bottle of Viagra."

"You know this, how?

"Peaches wasn't the first stripper to be involved with Zimmerman. I've represented a few who tried to get the pole up without luck, so he gave up and just had women around for show. He never loved Peaches. She was, as you said, eye-candy."

*

Chapter 17

I was about to start talking to Grisler about his involvement with any criminals who might want to murder him when my cell phone buzzed. According to my caller ID, it was Deacon. I stood, excusing myself from Grisler, and went past Louis to the hallway.

"Hey, Dad, what's up?" I asked with a smile.

"They're dropping like flies now. Another shyster was murdered about an hour ago. Harvey Goodwin. This is getting epidemic. Now the mayor's office is calling Weber and complaining. I don't know what they expect us to do, put all of the lawyers in protective custody and lock them up?" He sounded annoyed.

"I'd like to see that. Maybe leave them in jail for a good long time. Where are you?"

"I just left Lynn and the baby, and I'm heading to the crime scene. I'll text you the address if you want to come."

"Do that. I'm with Grisler and he's trying to hire me to help a stripper beat a murder rap. I'll wait for your text." I hung up and waited for the message to come through. I went back to Grisler and said, "Did you know a Harvey Goodwin?"

"Oh, crap, is he dead too? I never liked the guy, but I didn't want to see him murdered. When?"

"About an hour ago. I'll alert Louis and the other cop to be especially cautious with you." I turned and went back out in the hall where Louis and his partner were talking.

"Hey, guys, another lawyer was murdered. Keep a close eye on Grisler. The mayor is now getting involved with complaints. You know Weber is going to have fits."

Louis said, "When doesn't Weber have fits? We'll watch him closely."

"Thanks, I'll probably be back later."

"Are you taking the stripper's case?" Louis asked.

"I probably will have one of my associates handle it. I'm more involved with finding out who's killing all the lawyers."

"Yeah, well, don't rush. We could stand to cull the herd a bit," the other cop said.

I laughed and agreed. I left them and went back to my car. In the parking lot I saw Peaches talking to some guy. Probably a customer from the club who recognized her. I watched them for a moment until the man went off. Peaches got into a '61 T-bird that had plates saying "APZAWRK," and I thought on what it meant. She pulled out and sped off. Then it hit me, "A piece of work" was the meaning. Yes, she was a piece of work, in the good sense, I guessed. I smiled and went to my car.

I drove to the building where Deacon's text address sent me. It was down in Henderson, a nice new building with offices for professions from doctors to lawyers with a few insurance offices thrown in. I went through the tangle of cop cars, past the coroner's van, and into the building.

Deacon was standing in the hallway with a couple of suits. They looked like lawyers and were looking worried. Deacon nodded to me as I came up.

"Jim, this is Don Bartles and Frank Jaymes, lawyers. They have offices here in the building, and they think they saw the killer."

The one man Deacon pointed to as being Bartles said, "We were coming out of my office to go get something to eat when we ran into this sleazy looking guy coming from Harvey's office. We're used to the lower class of people here since we represent them. But I thought he was acting more like he wanted to get away from the place, not looking for a lawyer."

Deacon said, "I've got a sketch artist coming to get a description. Maybe a good break in the case. If he's in the system we'll find him."

I looked back at Bartles and asked, "You say he looked sleazy. I don't think it's the way a professional hit man would look? Would you agree?"

The men looked at each other, and then Jaymes said, "He didn't look like a high priced hit man, no. He could have been a junkie hired to kill Harvey, though. They'd do that for a fix."

"Yes, they would. But the other lawyers who were murdered were done professionally. Explosions, a shot to the head and careful gunshots through a door that took out Harold Skinner. This wasn't a nervous junkie working for a fix." I turned to Deacon and asked, "How was Harvey killed?"

"Throat cut, from what Joe Lang says. Not something that can be done without surprise. Joe said he didn't defend himself, so I'd say the killer got him when he wasn't looking."

"Or trusted him enough to let him that close. Did Joe say if it was from behind?"

"The CSI blood spatter tech says it was from behind. The blood shot out to his front on his desk."

"So the killer walked around behind him and slit his throat?" I said.

"Looking that way. I'll know better when I get all the reports in."

Jaymes spoke. "Should we start worrying about this? I mean, three lawyers were murdered and Grisler is in the hospital. Are we all subject to murder?"

"I hate to use the term but so far all the lawyers who were killed were what I consider to be…shysters," Deacon said.

The two men stiffened. Bartles said, "Not a term we like, but yes, they were the lower class of lawyers. Even Harvey was the black sheep of this building. We tolerated his abrasiveness, and he was an annoying little weasel. Not to speak ill of the dead."

"Well, if you two aren't shysters, then maybe you're safe," I said. They didn't smile, they just thanked us and walked off. Deacon called to them to stay around for the sketch artist.

"We have to find who's behind this," Deacon said. "Weber's on my butt now, and I don't like it."

"Let's see what the sketch comes up with and go from there. The sketch will be of the hit man, but if we can find him, maybe we can find out who hired him."

"I hope so."

"So how are Lynn and the baby doing?"

"She's fine, a little drowsy from the drugs to help her heal, and the baby is all pink and cute," the proud father said.

"I don't think you'll need me for a while. I need to go see Trapper about a stripper," I said with a grin.

"You said that on the phone. What's that about?"

"Grisler has a client who's going to be accused of murdering her married boyfriend, Robert Dillon-Zimmerman," I said. Deacon gave me a blank stare, so I explained who he was.

"Okay, I know who you're talking about now. The old fart who hangs with young babes. So your stripper thought he loved her and now he's dead. The police talking to the wife?"

"From what I hear. I'm having Trapper take it. I'm now really curious as to who's murdering lawyers. I'd like to shake his hand."

"You can be mean when you want." Deacon laughed.

"Especially when it comes to lawyers. I'm heading to my office. If you get a break, call."

"I will," he said, and I left him.

I drove back to my office but called Lacey to be sure Trapper was in. She said he was. I told her to tell him to wait for me and hung up. I arrived and parked, going in the back door, clanging the cow bell so Lacey would know I arrived. I went straight to Trapper's office and found him looking out his window.

"There's no escape that way, the windows don't open," I said as I came in.

He looked back at me and said, "They do too open. What was so hot you had me wait for you?"

“Hot is the word. A sultry red head who’s an exotic dancer,” I said with a grin.

“Okay, you have my undivided attention, talk to me.”

He went to his desk chair and I sat in his client chair. I explained the whole situation to him and he sat nodding. The grin on his face was getting wider.

“So you want me to investigate her case?” he said.

“Just her case, leave the body alone. I don’t know who’s in charge of the investigation, but you know every cop in Vegas, so it should be easy for you to find out.”

“I’ll get on it right away. Did she give you a number to call her?”

“No, but she dances at the Golden Shoe. I’m sure you can find her. Look for her car in the parking lot. A ’61 T-Bird with the plates that say, "APZAWRK." You figure it out."

*

Chapter 18

"Piece of work," he said.

"Quick you are, young Jedi," I said, like Yoda from Star wars.

"You say she's good looking?"

"Does that matter? She may become a client, not a date."

"I just like to know." He had an evil smile. "So Zimmerman is well-known. It should have made the papers, but I didn't see it today. I'll call around and see who has the case and get the facts. Are we taking the job or are you leaving it up to me to decide if it's worth it?"

"I know you don't like Grisler, but he's agreed to pay, so take the case. It can't hurt to look into it. I'm going up front to see what surprises Lacey has for me today. Let me know what happens." I stood and headed to the door.

"I'll get right on it," Trapper said as I left his office. I went up the hallway and saw that Buck was in. I hadn't seen him in a while so I stopped.

"You're still alive I see," I said.

"Barely, man. I have a good group of men who work hard but there are always a few who make my life miserable. I've been doing double time trying to get them to work."

"Fire them and get new men. With the economy, there are a lot of people who want a job," I said.

"Yeah, but there are too many out there with specialized skills that don't want to work as a security guard. And if they did, they'd quit as soon as something better came along. The unskilled labor ends up being goof offs or too lazy to work. I almost regret getting into this mess."

"Why don't you hire someone to manage the company? You could just sit around relaxing and watching them work."

Buck sat for a moment, thinking. "Hmm…not a bad idea. I'll give it some thought."

"You could let Mac take over, with a good pay raise. Lacey would like that."

"Yeah, Mac is dependable and knows the ropes. I'll have a talk with him and see what he thinks of the idea. Maybe I'll make him a junior partner. Give him some incentive to build the business."

"Good thinking. I'll talk to you later. I have to see what Lacey has for me." We said our good-byes and I left his office.

I went through the double glass doors half expecting Penny to attack me, but she didn't. I remembered that she was going to visit Lynn when she got done with her show.

"Nice to see you," Lacey said when I came to the counter.

"Nice to see you, too," I replied. "Got anything interesting for me?"

"Nope. Have you caught the killer yet?"

"Deacon and I are working on it."

"Well, you have to hurry. The newspapers are not treating the police nicely. They say that the police should be watching the lawyers better than they are."

"We can't watch all the lawyers, there's too many of them slinking under every rock in Clark County. Besides the lawyers should be watching out for themselves. They were warned."

"Either way, I wouldn't want to be a lawyer."

"You'd be a good lawyer. You're ruthless and you ask the right questions."

"Questions like, when are you going to turn in your monthly reports?"

"Okay, I'll get them to you soon." I smiled and went back to my office where it was quiet. I pulled out my report sheets. Might as well get them done. I had been working on them for about a half hour when Trapper came in and sat.

"I did some calling and found out who's in charge of the murder of Zimmerman. An old nemesis of mine, Walt Hartley. He's uptown now and pulled the case. I talked to him, and he was cordial but not helpful. He said the case is ongoing and none of my business. That's all right. I'm a good friend with his captain. We rode street bike patrol together years back. I'll get the info on our dead record man."

"You always have an ace up your sleeve, don't you? Find out what you can then call Grisler's personal secretary and get a retainer. When are you going to talk to Peaches?"

"Soon as possible. I'm heading for the Golden Shoe shortly."

"You pay your own tab there, no using petty cash. You'll drop a fortune on the strippers," I said.

“I always pay my own way. But I usually don’t get charged. It’s my fate to have all the women fall for me.”

“Dream on. Do you have your expense report ready for Lacey?”

“I’ll fill it out after I return from the Golden Shoe.” He stood and went out with a big grin.

“Remember what I said,” I yelled to him as he left my office. I knew he wouldn’t.

My desk phone startled me. I answered. “Hello, Jim Richards here.” It was Deacon. “Why didn’t you call me on my cell phone?”

“Your phone is shut off. You need to take care of that,” he said. “What are you doing?”

“Paperwork. I knew I shouldn’t have come into the office. What’s up?” I said as I turned the stupid phone on.

“Got the artist sketch and a hit in the system. Care to come in and help figure out how to nab the guy?”

“I’m leaving the office right now. Later.” I hung up and headed for the door. Lacey came around the corner and asked if I had my reports.

"I'm almost done, but Deacon called and they have an ID on the killer. He needs me."

"Anything to avoid doing it. Okay, go play detective and get yourself in the newspapers again. Maybe it will bring in more business."

I laughed and kissed her on the forehead. I was walking to the back door as she yelled, "That can be construed as sexual harassment. I'm filing a report."

"Good, do my reports while you're at it," I said as I went out.

I got in my car and drove to the precinct, parked and went in. Deacon was talking to Warren in the squad room. He saw me and waved.

"So, what's the progress?" I asked as I came up.

"Warren got an address of this guy. He's probably not going to be there, but it's worth a look."

"So Vegas hit men have addresses in the city that we can get to?"

"I know, it baffles me, too. But he has a driver's license, and he had to put an address on it. The address is listed so it's legit." He handed me the sketch and the printout of the driver's license. "Let's go see if we can nab him."

Deacon told Warren to follow in his car in case we needed backup. The three of us left and went to our cars. We headed out Charleston to a subdivision almost out of the city. This was an apartment building on Charleston at the entrance to the subdivision. We pulled in with Warren right behind.

Deacon said to me, "I'd like you to hold back in case this gets out of hand. If this guy is a pro, he could be dangerous."

I looked at the building. "Which apartment is he in?"

Deacon looked at the paper he had and then at the building. "The one in the middle on the ground floor."

The building had three up and three down on the side we were on. I was sure there were more behind this side.

"Okay, I'll stay back by the cars. I can at least see you guys. If it's clear, call to me."

"Will do. Here we go." Deacon got out, Warren joined him and they went to the door. Deacon banged on it and they waited. I could see them clearly while I stood next to the car with my hand on my Glock in case.

They waited, then Deacon started banging again, identifying them as cops. I saw Warren go to the window and look in. He stood up and motioned to Deacon who came to look in the window also. Deacon straightened and went to the door. He brought his foot up and hit the door. It didn't budge the first time so he hit it again. It flew open and they went in.

I left the car and came up to the opening. Deacon and Warren were kneeling down looking at the body on the floor in a pool of blood. Deacon looked at me and said, "It's our killer."

*

Chapter 19

Joe Lang proclaimed the cause of death to have been a slit throat. That caused Deacon to be concerned since the last lawyer was murdered in the same way.

"It was done the same way, yes. The same way the knife was pulled across the throat in both cases, from behind. This man was possibly murdered by the unsub in the Goodwin death," Joe said.

"So there's another hit man who killed this guy?" Deacon said.

"Or it was the person who hired the hit man. Maybe he ran out of money or maybe this vic wanted more money to keep quiet," I said.

"Anything is possible. How's the baby doing, Deacon?" Joe asked.

"Real good. She's pink and cute and looks just like Lynn," Deacon said puffing out his chest.

"Good thing she doesn't look like you. Now that would be an ugly baby." Joe laughed as he followed his men who were pushing the gurney with the body in the bag.

"Everyone is a comedian," Deacon muttered and went into the apartment again. CSI was still going over the room where the vic died.

"Larry, do you have anything yet?"

The CSI supervisor smiled and said, "Deacon, we are forensic techs, not magicians. The guy is identified as Wilbur Reese. Give us a little time; we'll have something more for you. I have to say, this guy was clumsy. We do have some good evidence, and we'll process it before releasing the facts. You are a nervous father."

"I'm new to the maternity thing. Get back to me as soon as possible. Thanks." Deacon spun and left the room, going out to the parking lot. I followed.

"All we can do is wait. I'm wearing down, it's been a long day. I'm going back to sit with Lynn and hold her hand. You should visit when you can. She asked for you," Deacon said as he slipped into the car.

"I think Penny went to visit her this afternoon. I'll stop by later. I'm getting tired, too, so take me to my car and we'll go at this again tomorrow."

Deacon dropped me at my car and drove off. I drove out and back home. Penny's car was in the garage as I pulled in. I wasn't going back out tonight if possible. I came into the kitchen and Willy bounced around my feet. I picked him up and hugged him.

"How's my little boy?" I asked him.

Penny came in and asked, "Who are you talking to?"

"Who else, our son." I smiled and held the dog out to her.

She took him and gave me a kiss. "Get dressed, we have a dinner date." She left the kitchen while I wondered what she was talking about. I followed.

"Dinner date? With who?" I asked as I entered the bedroom where she was going through the closet picking out clothes.

"Earl and Paula. They were at the hospital visiting Lynn and the baby. We were talking about Angelo's restaurant and made plans for dinner. I hoped you'd be back before it got too late. Now get dressed, something nice."

I sat on the edge of the bed, wanting to take a nap, but she was throwing clothes at me to wear. "Okay, stop throwing my stuff."

"If I don't, you'll dress funny." She left the room, leaving me alone.

I got dressed after throwing water on my face and shaving. I woke a little more and went out to find Penny in the kitchen pouring a glass of wine.

"Wine this early? Are you becoming an alcoholic?"

"No, just something to brace myself. You and Earl will bore Paula and me with shop talk."

I went to the cupboard, got out a glass and opened a beer. I poured about a half glass and toasted her.

"Now who's an alcoholic?" she asked.

"What? A half glass of beer to brace me when you and Paula start talking about fashion."

She whacked my arm and left the kitchen. I stood looking at Willy on the floor. "What? Do you want a bracer, too?" I picked his bowl up and ran water into it. I set it down and he lapped it up.

Penny came back in and asked if I was ready to go. "No, I've had a long day and didn't get my nap."

"You haven't had a nap in months, so don't use that excuse. Now let's step it up, before they start without us."

We went to the garage and took Penny's car. I let her drive so I could nap on the way. She kept hitting my arm, keeping me awake.

"You're a mean woman. I don't know why I married you."

"Because you love me. And I'm such a great catch." She gave her evil little smile. "Plus I'm great in bed."

"I'll agree with that last part. I only use you for sex."

We arrived at Angelo's restaurant and parked. Earl was standing just inside the entrance talking to Angelo. They both welcomed me.

"Mr. R, how's everything?" Angelo asked.

"I'm doing well, my friend."

"Mrs. R, I hear your show is going back to the network."

"That's correct, Angelo. It will be sometime in the next few weeks. I'll be sure to get you in to watch the first show," Penny said.

"Thanks, Mrs. R, that would be real nice."

"Hey, Earl," I said. "Have you gotten any dirt on Grisler?"

"Are you still wanting me to do that? You asked me a long time ago to bring him down. Now he's in the hospital at death's door and you still want me to get him convicted?"

"Now that you say it that way, I guess we can forget it. But maybe in your explorations you may find out who wants to murder him."

"What about the other lawyers? It sounds like this is a serial killer with a goal."

"I agree, but I have agreed to find the killer. We had a suspect, but he was murdered."

"Really? You have a killer killing killers?" Earl asked.

Penny stepped in between us and asked, "Where's Paula. I need to get away from you two."

Angelo laughed and took Penny's arm. "Follow me and I'll take you to the table." They went into the dining room, leaving Earl and me alone.

"You don't think we go overboard on our cases, do you?" I asked.

"Of course not. We do our jobs and do them well. Okay, not all the time, but most. Shall we go eat?" he said and went to the dining room followed by me.

We had a great meal. My new daughter, Carol, had prepared it. I thought she was working too hard, but she said she loved the job and didn't mind the hours. Besides, she was making good money now. Angelo made sure her pay was on par with the best chefs in Vegas. He didn't want a rival restaurant stealing her away.

We finished our dinner and then, after saying our good-byes to Angelo, we went to the Venetian Hotel to the lounge to listen to the band.

We talked and danced until about midnight when we decided to call it a night. I quietly asked Earl to continue his checking of Grisler. I thought it might help us to find the killer. He agreed.

Penny drove back. I had a few too many beers. Las Vegas is sort of tolerant of drivers who have been drinking. Everyone did it. But I wasn't going to push my luck.

We arrived home and fed Willy who was not happy we left him alone. I could tell.

We crawled into bed and snuggled.

"Now, you were saying something earlier about how you only keep me for the sex?" Penny said in my ear.

"I did," I replied, anticipating.

"Well, I hope you dream about that great sex," she said, laughed and turned over, snuggling her back to me. We spooned.

I fell asleep a short time after Penny did. I was thinking about Grisler, about the little weasel lying in the hospital bed. Then I thought about Peaches LaFarge, Grisler's client. She was a good looking woman for her occupation. Maybe Trapper could help her. I was dreaming about being in a large room with coffins all filled with lawyers. I kept seeing a dark shadow moving around the room. Every time I turned to see who was behind me, the shadow vanished. I wasn't happy.

Early next morning Penny was getting ready to go to work, if one could call it work. I'd like to sit and talk to people and have my questions shown on TV. Oh, well.

Penny kissed me, took Willy with her and left. I ate my toast in silence. My cell phone suddenly shook me out of my peaceful reverie. It was Deacon. I hated to answer it because it probably meant someone, maybe Grisler, was dead.

*

Chapter 20

"Hey, Pop, what's up?" I responded to the call.

"We got another dead lawyer," came the reply.

"Grisler?" I asked.

"Unfortunately, no." He laughed.

"Okay, are you there?"

"No, they just called me. The vic is out in Sommerlin. It's not my jurisdiction, but they knew I was investigating murders of lawyers. Jim, this guy wasn't a shyster. I think maybe we have a copycat. Now even the good lawyers aren't safe."

"Sommerlin. That's some fancy community. I understand the Howard Hughes Corporation built it," I said.

"Yeah, they had a hand in it. You want to join me?" Deacon asked.

"Of course. Just to get a chance to go out there, sure. I'll be in shortly," I said and hung up. I dropped the last of my toast in the trash can and grabbed my things to go. I was out the door and in my car in record time.

I arrived at the precinct and found Deacon standing in the parking lot talking to some man in a black suit. FBI? I parked and went over to them.

"Jim, this is agent Sam Harris, FBI." I was right. Deacon continued, "The lawyer murdered today was a federal prosecutor. So we have the FBI involved now."

I shook the hand of the Feebie and smiled. He turned back to Deacon. "I'll need your cooperation by giving me copies of the murder facts of the other lawyers. It could be connected to this case."

"I'll have them to you by the end of the day," Deacon said. Agent Harris thanked him and nodded to me then walked off.

"Don't ask me why, but I don't like that man," Deacon said.

"He's from a different world of law enforcement than you. He's an alien in your world. Now what do we have on this new murder?" I asked.

"Not much. The lead on the case, Paul Sutter, called me and gave me what he could before the FBI stepped in and took over."

"Strange the FBI got there so quickly," I said.

"I was wondering about that also. The lawyer was murdered sometime around six this morning. How did they get here so fast? Did they have some info before the murder?"

"The Feebies have an office here in Vegas?"

"They do, but they must have been watching our channels to find out about the kill and who it was. They must have key words on their spy devices that send an alarm when one of their federal people is killed."

"Can we still go to the crime scene?"

"I'd like to see them stop me, if they want my cooperation. Let's go." He turned and went to the unmarked cop car parked by the curb. We drove up and over to Sommerlin. The master-planned community is in the Las Vegas Valley near the Spring Mountains and Red Rock Canyon National Conservation Area. It lies partially within the city limits of Las Vegas and in unincorporated Clark County. It was named for Howard Hughes' grandmother, Jean Amelia Summerlin. It holds about 100,000 people and is a pretty ritzy community. I had never been there so this was a good chance to see the place and maybe go into a house.

We arrived and parked outside the house which was busy with both cop cars and FBI SUVs. Deacon pointed out Paul Sutter, the lead detective. We approached him as he was quietly arguing with a suit.

Paul was speaking. "I don't care where your jurisdiction is. I also wouldn't care if he was the president of Uganda, this will be my case. I'm sorry he was a Fed, go talk to someone who cares."

Paul stood about a head taller than the Fed and about a hundred pounds bigger. The suit just stared and then turned away. "I'll be back with your captain," he swore as he walked away.

Paul turned to Deacon and welcomed him. “Deacon, the new daddy. Is your daughter dating yet?”

“Don’t start on that. I’ll have her locked up until she collects social security. Now what’s the deal here?”

“The vic was not one of your shyster lawyers. He was a Fed lawyer attached to the Clark County organized crime task force. The Feds think it was a mob hit so it doesn’t ring true for your murders. But since he was a murdered lawyer, I thought you might want to come see what we have.”

“Yeah, none of my lawyers had anything to do with mob cases. I think this may be an unrelated case. I hope you can play nice with the Feds,” Deacon said with a laugh.

“I’m a school yard bully. They better come at me in numbers. If you want to go see the crime scene, talk to the CSI lead.”

“Thanks, Paul. Good luck,” Deacon said, and we headed to the house.

It was a very big and expensive looking place. The back overlooked the first hole of the Palm Valley Golf Course. I think it was the first hole. My eyesight is not as sharp as it used to be to see the flag on the pin.

We entered the building to find Larry, the CSI supervisor. "Larry, what are you doing out here?" Deacon asked.

"We're running thin again, so I go where they send me. I don't mind since I get to see the golf course."

"You like golf? I could never figure out that game. Walking around all day hitting your balls."

"Better than football and having your balls hit," he said with a smile.

"Hey, there's more to football than having your balls hit. Now what do you have so far?"

"Cause of death was sharp force trauma. Looks like a pointed object hit his skull from behind. We're searching for the weapon, but it could be out in a waterhole on the golf course. We won't know what kind of weapon until Joe Lang checks the body."

"These lawyers are keeping Joe busy." Deacon laughed.

We were interrupted by a woman demanding to come in. The officer at the door was keeping her out. Paul came up from outside to see what the commotion was about. We went to the door, and Larry went off to the crime scene.

"Let me in. He's my brother! What happened? All these police cars, is he all right?" She was hysterical.

Paul pulled her aside, away from the frazzled officer. We came up as he was trying to calm her.

"Who are you, besides the victim's sister?" Paul asked.

"Victim! Why is he a victim? What happened?" she screamed.

"Calm down and I'll tell you. Calm down now or I'll have an officer put you in a patrol car."

She took a breath and stood up straight. "I'm sorry. Now tell me what happened?"

"We can't say right now. We're investigating. When we have something for you, we'll tell you. All I can say is he's dead, and if you know who may have wanted to hurt him, talk to me now."

"I didn't involve myself with his job. I can't help you. Sorry." She composed herself and quieted.

We all turned to see Joe Lang coming up the walk with his crew. Paul excused himself from the sister and went to him. We stood just behind the woman.

She looked back to us and said, "Who's the hunk who just came up?"

We were a bit surprised by her turnaround. Deacon said, "Joe Lang."

"Hmm…is he a cop?" she mumbled.

Joe turned to his men with his back now to us. The back of his jacket said in big letters, Clark County Coroner. The sister turned back to us and said, "No, thank you. I don't need a man who deals with death." Then she walked off.

"She's an odd one." Paul came back to us, and Deacon told him about the woman's change of temperament. He said he'd check her out. She could be a suspect.

"If you come up with anything useful, call me," Deacon said, and Paul replied that he would.

Deacon motioned to me that he wanted to leave. We did. In the car driving back to the precinct Deacon laughed. "I run into the strangest people."

"I hope you're not referring to me," I said.

"No, I knew you were strange from the day I met you back in Penny's studio in Michigan. I'm talking about the weirdoes here in Vegas. I guess since this place is called Sin City it comes with the territory."

"Michigan was boring, wouldn't you say?"

"I don't know, there were strange people back there, too. Just had to know where to look. That's where I found you," he said with a grin.

*

Chapter 21

Trapper had gone to the Golden Shoe only to find out that Peaches wasn't working for a couple days. He couldn't get anyone to tell him where to find her and he didn't want to call the investigating detective since they weren't good friends. In fact they were not friends at all. He was one of the very few cops Trapper disliked with a passion.

He thought about going to visit Grisler in the hospital to see if he had an address for her, but he wasn't fond of Grisler either. Come to think of it, he wasn't fond of a lot of people.

Trapper drove to the hospital and went up to Grisler's room. He had a hard time getting the location, but after showing his investigator's ID, they reluctantly told him where to find the room. He had less trouble getting past the cop at the door. Trapper's reputation preceded him, and the cop knew who he was.

"Trapper, good to see you again. It's been a long time. How you been?" the cop said.

"Ken, good to see you, too. I've been good. I'm working private now with Jim Richards."

"I heard that you were back in town and hooked up with Richards. Good move. Are you here to see Grisler?"

"Not that I want to, but yes. Is he awake?"

"Oh, he certainly is. He's with some red-head. A real fox and, as I understand, a stripper."

"Well, that saves me a lot of running around. She's the person I'm looking for. I figured Grisler would know where she is."

"Your lucky day. I'd like to find her too."

"Ken, you wouldn't know what to do with her if you had her."

The cop punched Trapper kiddingly on the arm, and Trapper went into the room. Grisler was sitting up in bed, and Peaches was in the chair next to him. The shyster looked surprised to see Trapper, probably because he had been involved in the Carlos Hernandez murder case.

"Well, if it isn't Will Trapper, investigator supreme. What brings you to my humble abode?"

"Abode? Are you setting up office here now? An ambulance chaser living in the hospital. That's clever."

"Now that you mention it, yes, it is. I'll need to have my secretary bring me my business cards to hand out to the patients. Now what do you want?"

"I certainly don't want you. It's your friend here I'm interested in. Jim Richards sent me to take her case." He went to the woman and held out his hand. She took it and smiled.

"I'm Will Trapper. As Alphonse said, investigator supreme. I work with Jim Richards. Pleasure to meet you."

Peaches gave him a bigger smile and said, "Are you going to keep me from being involved in Bobby's murder?"

"If by Bobby, you mean Robert Dillon-Zimmerman, yes. I'm going to try to keep you from being involved. Now we need to talk."

She giggled and said, “Well, my lawyer is present, so I guess I can talk.”

Trapper grimaced and said, “You don’t need your lawyer while you're talking to me. I’m on your side and I’m not the police. Now I prefer to talk in private,” he said and looked at Grisler. “No offence.”

“None taken. I’m tired of listening to her anyway,” he said.

“Al, are you tired of me?”

“Peachy dear, you have a habit of talking in circles.” He looked at Trapper. “She’s yours. Good luck.”

Trapper smiled, took Peaches’ hand and pulled her up. “We’ll be out in the waiting lounge.” He led her out of the room as the cop was checking her out. Trapper winked at the cop, and he and Peaches went to the lounge down the hall. It was empty, so they were alone. Trapper sat her by the window and sat next to her on the couch.

“Now tell me about yourself,” he said.

“What do you want to know? About myself, I’m a girl from LA and I have a mother and a father still there. I have two adult brothers who are still living at home with my parents. One is in dental school and the other is on parole. He was caught stealing jewelry by an off-duty cop in a department store. Wal-Mart, to be exact. He got two years and, because of overcrowding, they let him out after six months. But he's had a run of bad luck. Now he's trying to get straight by going to night school and getting his GED. He hopes to get an office job, working for an insurance company that promised him they'd teach him how to sell insurance. But he needs a high school diploma and three hundred dollars for the course."

Trapper's head was starting to hurt. "Peaches, stop. Let me ask you a few questions now." He waited for her to acknowledge him, but she seemed distant. "Hello, anyone home?" he asked.

"I don't know. Who's home?"

"It's an expression. Sorry, I don't want to confuse you. Now how did you meet...Bobby?"

"Oh, he would come into the club and put dollars in my thong. He liked to have me give him lap dances, but the poor man couldn't get it up. So he just enjoyed the rubbing. If you know what I mean."

"Oh, I do."

"Well, one night he came in and explained how he wanted to have me be his date to some party his record company was putting on. I thought it would be good to meet all the big singers his company represented, so I said yes. Well, after that night he had me go with him all over the city. We would go to clubs and parties being put on by his company. Then he asked me to be his girlfriend. I said sure. He was fun and would buy me expensive jewelry, which my brother tried to pawn. I was falling for Bobby, even though he was still married. But they were getting divorced, so I figured it was okay."

Trapper stopped her again. "Okay, what happened to Bobby? How did he die?"

"He was taking a soak and somehow a radio fell into the tub and electrocuted him."

"Why would he have a radio in his bathroom?" Deacon asked.

"Oh, he wasn't in his bathroom. He was on his porch in his hot tub."

"Oh, that kind of tub. Still, why would he have a radio next to his tub where it could fall and kill him?"

"He never did before. I don't know why he did that night."

"You knew he didn't have one before that night? How many times had you been in the tub with him?"

"Oh, lots of times. We would be in the tub two, maybe three times a week. He couldn't have sex, but he liked to watch my wet body. I wasn't there the night he died. I was dancing."

"Wait, you were dancing the night he died?"

"Yeah. I had to work and told him I couldn't spend my usual Wednesday night with him."

"Who else knew you had to work?"

"I don't know, just Bobby. He's the only one I told."

"Okay, probably why you haven't been called in to be questioned if you were working. I suppose you were seen by everyone at the club that night. Were you there all night, never left at any time?"

"No, I was dancing doubles because we were short on dancers. I never rested."

"I don't think they'll look at you for murder. If it was murder. Did Bobby like to listen to the radio?"

"Not really. He was in the record business and got enough music to give him fits, or so he said."

Trapper sat for a moment thinking. "Okay, I'll talk to the detective in charge and see what they have. You may still be called in to be questioned. Just tell them exactly what you told me. I'm sure they'll be glad to let you go."

"Thank you, Mr. Trapper. I feel so much better."

"Good, now I'll take you back to Grisler. He deserves you." Trapper laughed to himself and led her back to the room. He went by his friend at the door and winked again. Peaches went into the room, and Trapper left.

Out at his Jeep in the hospital parking he stood thinking again. In years past he had lots of hookers and strippers as friends, but this one was different. She was honest and open. A bit scattered, but not bad. Trapper's relationship with Samantha was cooling to the point that they hardly saw each other, so he thought maybe now that Bobby was out of the picture, he might ask Peaches out.

*

Chapter 22

Deacon and I were back in Lynn's office when Deacon got a call on his cell phone. He answered and listened for a moment. "Thanks, that's great to hear." He hung up and sat back in his chair. "That was forensics. The killer of Harold Skinner, the one who was shot through the door, was caught on a camera from the bank across the street. Forensics managed to enhance the video, and it was our dead suspect, Wilbur Reese. Now we know he did the crime, but we need to find out who murdered him and why. I'll get Warren to run this Wilbur Reese and see if he was taking under the table. Forensics also said the unsub who murdered Reese left a few bits of trace, and they are working on that."

"So Reese was our killer up to his death. Reese must have slit the throat of that lawyer…I've lost track of the names," I said.

"Don't ask me. I need a score card at this point," Deacon replied.

We were surprised to see Trapper come to the door. Deacon said, "Will, what are you doing out this way?"

"I need your influence with the North Vegas police." He looked at me and said, "I talked to Peaches and she has an air tight alibi for Zimmerman's murder. Deacon, can you can talk to the lead detective in the Zimmerman murder case and slip some info to him?"

"Sure, who you talking about?"

"Walt Hartley. He's an ass who I tolerated back when I ran with LVMPD. I just need to have you throw him a bone on the case." Trapper explained the whole details of Peaches' involvement and her alibi. "If you could let Hartley know Peaches was working that night, then he'll leave her alone."

Deacon sat back and grinned. "You just have a soft spot for the ladies, don't you? Especially hookers and strippers."

"They are misunderstood. Most of them have goals to improve themselves, and society brands them as less than trash because they take off their clothes. Wives do that all the time in private for husbands or lovers."

"Okay, I'll call. You owe me." Deacon picked up the desk phone and started to dial. "Now if I didn't waste all those hours in actor school…uh, yeah, Detective DeAngelo, LVMP South, may I talk to Walt Hartley…thanks." He was quiet for a few minutes, smiling at us.

"Yeah, Hartley, how you doing? Deacon DeAngelo here." He listened, then continued. "I had the Richards Investigation firm contact me to see who was in charge of the Zimmerman case. I found out you were. How's it going?" He listened some more. "Well, Richards was hired to check out Peaches LaFarge for Alphonse Grisler, her lawyer. He was concerned his client would be a suspect in the murder. Richards' people investigated and found that the woman was working the night of the murder and has dozens of witnesses who can verify she was working." He listened some more and then smiled. "That's great. I'll pass that on to Grisler. Thanks so much." He hung up.

"Well, Peaches is definitely off the hook. Your case is over. Hartley confirmed that the wife murdered Zimmerman. Finger prints all over the murder weapon. The radio helped to convince her to confess."

I looked at Trapper. "Well, that was a quick case. Make sure you bill Grisler for your time, as short as it was."

Trapper grinned, stood, then said, "I have some more investigating to do. I'm not finished."

"Oh, hell, you're going to try to get your hands on Peaches, aren't you?" I said.

He smiled again and thanked Deacon, then left.

"He's going to regret getting close to these women one day," I said.

Deacon's phone rang again and he answered. He listened and hung up. He wasn't smiling.

"Another lawyer dead?" I asked.

"No, this time it's a judge. And I'm sure we will be hearing from the mayor's office and Weber. Jim, we got to get this solved and quickly."

"See if forensics has something on that trace, and get Warren on the financials and background of Reese."

Deacon stood and went out of the office, going to Warren's desk. He leaned over to the detective and said something. Warren nodded, and Deacon came back. He sat at the desk and picked up the phone, dialed and waited.

"Larry, Deacon here. Please tell me you got something off the trace from Reese's crime scene." He waited then said, "Thanks." He hung up and looked at me. "They got prints off a door knob from someone who shouldn't have been there. Jason Franson, attorney at law. Grisler was right, he was after his job."

He stood and said, "I'll get an address of his office and we'll go see our new suspect." He left the room as I pulled out my cell phone. I called Penny to see how she was doing.

"Yes, may I speak to the lady of the house," I said when she answered. Of course, I'm sure she saw it was me on her caller ID.

"You better believe I'm the lady of the house. I also wear the pants. Now what political party are you soliciting for?"

"The Strippers for A Better World Party. We need more pole dancers, and I was wondering if you'd like to volunteer to teach people the art of the pole dance?"

"What do you want, Richards? I don't have time to goof around on the phone. I have a phone sex line to run."

"Are you making any money with it?"

"Hell, no. No one has any money to pay for phone sex anymore. How would you like to donate to the fund?"

"Sorry, I'm broke. My wife gets all my money."

"Ha! You wish. Where are you?"

"I'm in Lynn's office, waiting for Deacon to get an address for our suspect. Where are you?"

"I'm home with Willy. We're cooking some different meals that I learned today on my show."

"You're actually cooking? Who will you get to eat it?"

"You will when you get home. These are crock pot meals and can stay good for a long time. What time are you coming home?"

I looked at my watch. It was just after noon, and I figured I had about another hour of chasing down the suspect. He was a lawyer so it could be a long interrogation. I figured I could be home by five and that's what I told Penny.

"Good, I'll figure for then. If you aren't here by five, your dinner goes in the trash. Got that, buster?"

When she calls me buster, it's serious. "I'll be there if I have to bring the suspect with me."

"You better not," she said and hung up.

I sat back waiting for Deacon. He returned, picked up his jacket from the back of the chair and put it on. "You ready to go nab a lawyer?"

"Love to." We left the station and drove over to Flamingo by Durango. We found the office building. It was one story and mostly brick and chrome. It looked expensive and something a lawyer would love.

We parked on the side and went in. The secretary announced us, and the shark came out of his office and greeted us. Deacon had called for backup and two officers were standing by.

When Franson held out his hand to shake, Deacon slapped the cuffs on him and said, "Jason Franson, you are under arrest for suspicion of murder." He recited the Miranda and gave Franson to the officers to take to the waiting patrol car.

Franson was yelling that his civil rights were being infringed on and this was an illegal arrest. Deacon just said, "Tell it to your lawyer. Oh wait, you are a lawyer. Take him out of here."

Deacon waited until they had left the building then said to me, "I had Warren call the DA about a warrant to search this place. I don't know what we'll find but it could be interesting."

I turned to the secretary and said, "I think you can take the day off. Mr. Franson will be busy for a while." She looked distressed, but started getting her things to leave. She asked if we could close up after we were finished, and then she was gone.

Williams came in with the warrant and a couple officers. Deacon asked him to start searching and get back to him. He turned to me and said, "Shall we go shake Franson's tree and see what falls out?"

*

Chapter 23

As we were leaving the building, Deacon's cell phone buzzed. He answered and listened, did a bit of stammering in response and hung up.

"Crap. That was Weber. He insisted I go to the judge's house to investigate his murder. Since I'm on the shyster killings, he wants me to see if there's any connection. The judge probably was murdered by his wife."

"Who is this judge?" I asked.

"Judge Augustus Plumm. Very old and very mean. I've had to stand in his court to testify a few times, and it wasn't pleasant. I can think of any number of lawyers who'd want to kill him. I have to call Warren and tell him to hold Franson until I get there. He's going to be one pissed lawyer. Probably sue the department for unlawful incarceration."

We drove out to the judge's home and parked. CSI and the coroner, Joe Lang, were already on the scene. Deacon went up to another detective and asked if he was the primary on the scene.

"Yep, Deacon, I got lucky and drew the lead. Not that I want it, but it's my jurisdiction. Aren't you lucky?" the detective said.

"Jim Richards, this is Mitch Newberg, North Vegas' finest detective." Deacon laughed.

"Aren't you sweet? Good to finally put a face to the reputation, Jim. You seem to be in the news a lot." He turned to Deacon. "Want to see the crime scene?"

"May as well. Weber is on my tail about linking this with my lawyer murders."

He led us into the very nice house. We went down a long hallway and into what looked like a study or library. Books on every wall and a huge wooden desk in the middle of the room. One of the CSI techs brought over what he said was the murder weapon. I stared at it and started to laugh aloud.

"What's the matter with you?" Deacon asked me.

I was still laughing when I said, "Don't you realize that Judge Plumm was murdered in the library with the candlestick." I continued to laugh until Deacon hit my arm.

"Knock it off or get out," he said, then he started to chuckle. Then Newberg started to laugh.

We all were enjoying a laugh as the CSI tech shook his head and left the room with the heavy looking candlestick.

Deacon talked to Newberg a short time longer about what he knew and then, satisfied, we left.

“Shall I put in my report about the library, candlestick link?” Deacon said with a smirk.

“You should look into Col. Mustard also. He may be involved,” I replied.

We arrived back at the precinct and went in. Warren came over and said, “Franson is climbing the walls. I locked him in and left him to stew. He should be ready for you.”

“Thanks loads, Greg. I’ll do the same for you some day.” Deacon went to the interrogation room door and stopped. “I think you should stay out. These lawyers will find any way to screw up an interrogation, and since you are a civilian, you shouldn’t be in there.”

“No problem. The further I’m away from a lawyer, the better. Good luck,” I said and went to the observation room. I sat looking through the magic mirror at Franson who was pacing the room. I don’t think he liked small quarters. I hoped he could get used to a cell if Deacon could trip him up.

Deacon came through the door and pointed to a chair. Franson hesitated until Deacon said to sit, now. Franson reluctantly sat with Deacon sitting across from him.

"Mr. Franson, we meet again. How are you doing today?" Deacon said with a smile.

"Cut the crap, DeAngelo. This is bull pucky and you know it. I never murdered anyone."

"No, but you hired one Wilbur Reese to murder and attempt to murder lawyers like yourself. Shysters."

"Watch it, detective. Slander is a serious offence," he spit out.

"If the shoe fits. Now where were you yesterday around six in the morning?"

"I was sleeping, with my girlfriend. I got up around seven and got ready to go to work. She'll verify I was with her."

Deacon pushed a pad of paper to him. "Okay, give me her name and I'll have a talk with her."

Franson sat staring at the paper. "I'd like my phone call please."

"To whom, your lawyer or your girlfriend to establish an alibi?" Deacon smiled.

"I don't have to answer that, but yes, my lawyer," Franson said quietly.

"I'd like to know where this one phone call thing started. It doesn't make sense. Okay, sit here and after you write the name of your girlfriend, I'll let you make a call."

"I want my lawyer, now."

Deacon held his tongue, not wanting to strangle the man. "Okay, lawyer up. You know the drill. Sit here until I get your lawyer. If you'll write his name and your girlfriend's name I'll take care of that for you."

Franson just sat and said nothing more. Deacon couldn't interrogate him further since he invoked his lawyer rights. He stood and said, "Fine." Then he left the room.

I came out of observation as Deacon was swearing in the squad room. "Ass. I'll get him for the murder of every lawyer including the judge. Let him act like he's in charge. Damn, I wish Lynn was here."

"You did all you could do. He knows the game, and he's been playing it way too long. Maybe if he sits overnight he'll soften up," I said.

"I doubt it. I'm going to have Warren and Williams run a check on his bank to see if he's put out large amounts of money for a hitman. Maybe we could talk to Grisler since he knows this creep."

"Sounds good. Unfortunately, I have to depart from you. Penny has my dinner hovering over the trash. So you'll probably play around with him all night, I imagine."

"Yep, the wheels of justice will move very slowly tonight. He'll be here for a while."

We said our good-byes and I left. I was thinking on the way home about Franson. I didn't like the man and hoped he was the person who hired Reese to murder lawyers. But since Reese had been murdered, who murdered the judge? It had to be not related to our cases. Well, I'd have to worry about that later. My main worry now was what kind of food Penny had simmering for me when I got home.

I arrived and parked in the garage since I wasn't planning on going back out. At least I hoped I wouldn't have to go back out. I came into the kitchen and was delightfully surprised by the smell of food.

Penny was in the kitchen at the refrigerator door taking out a bottle of wine. She gave me a smile, the one I fell in love with. I went to her and kissed her as she put her arms around my neck, resting the cold bottle on the bare skin of my neck. I jumped and moved away.

"You did that deliberately, didn't you?" I said.

She smiled and went to get the cork screw. We didn't buy the type of wine with twist off caps or in boxes. Our wine cost about ten dollars more a bottle than the drug store wines. Not that we were snobs, but we could afford the good wines now.

"I'm glad you're here on time. That shows you are maturing," she said with a grin.

"Maturing? I'm sixty-three years old. Aren't I mature enough?"

"You're like a little child sometimes, but you're improving. Now sit down at the dining table and we'll eat. I slaved over the crock pot for hours and you will enjoy it."

I knew I had better. I sat at the table, and she pulled the ceramic pot from the heater and put it on the table. It smelled good. My mouth was watering so I hoped it would taste good.

"What is it?" I asked.

"Shepherd's Stew. An old recipe and easy to make. Now eat," she said and sat across from me. I dished out a good size pile of the meat and veggies.

I took a cautious bite of the food and was surprised. It was great. I started to wolf down some more. Penny told me to slow down. I did. I savored the meal and was happy.

*

Chapter 24

I enjoyed the food and was happy that Penny had added one more meal to her small list of dinners she could cook. I helped her clean the table and the dishes then we retired to the living room and sat on the couch. Penny brought our beer and chips, then I turned on the TV and we watched the local news.

The murder of the judge made the top of the news. They interviewed detective Mitch Newberg, and he was vague about the murder. I don't know why these reporters even ask about a case. The cops won't tell them anything. We watched a couple sitcoms and then went to bed. Willy was already on his Bates Motel easy chair, sleeping. I undressed and crawled in next to Penny.

"That was a great meal, babe. I'm proud that you're doing so well with the cuisine. Maybe you could have Carol come over and give you a few more lessons," I said.

She mulled that over then said, "That's not a bad idea. But don't get the idea that I'm going to be cooking you dinner every night." She smiled, kissed me on the nose and snuggled in for the night.

I was up earlier than Penny for once. She was still sleeping peacefully when I quietly went out of the bedroom to the kitchen. Willy was right at my feet, patiently waiting for his breakfast. I poured his kibble in the bowl, and he went at it. For such a small dog he could wolf down his food.

"Slow down, that's all you're getting," I said as Penny came stumbling into the room.

"Slow who down?" she asked groggily.

"I was talking to Willy. He eats too fast."

"He has a fast metabolism. What's on your agenda today?" she asked.

"I guess I'm going to watch Deacon interrogate a lawyer. He may be our suspect in all the murders."

"You really should visit with Lynn. She asks about you."

"I will fit it in today, definitely."

"You better. The baby is so cute, you should see her before she graduates from high school. Oh, and I volunteered us to baby sit when Lynn gets out of the hospital so Deacon can take her out to a nice dinner."

"I'll even pay for it. I'll tell them to go to Angelo's, and I'll tell Angelo to give them the full treatment."

"That would be nice. You mention it to Lynn when you go visit. I'll stop by after I get done with my show today. Got to get ready," she said and went back to the bedroom. I was surprised she didn't make her oatmeal.

"Make me breakfast, please," she yelled from the hallway.

"Okay, I should have seen that coming," I said to Willy as he looked up at me.

Penny and Willy had departed, and I was on my way to see Deacon beat his suspect. I arrived and parked, saying hi to the officer at the back entrance. He gave me his creepy smile again. I had to find out what that was about.

Deacon was in the squad room, stomping around while Weber stood talking to some suit. I got closer to hear what they were saying, but far enough to remain invisible.

"I don't care what you want. This man is our suspect and we will interrogate him," Weber yelled at the man.

"I'm sorry, Captain, but we will be taking him for our investigation. Talk to your chief. He has already been informed."

"This is bull. I will go to the top!" Weber yelled .

Two more suits came and took Franson out of the interrogation room then led him, handcuffed, out the back door. I watched from the side as Deacon sat in a chair by Warren's desk.

"I give up. Just when we get a good lead, the FBI screws us over. This guy had nothing to do with that federal lawyer. He wasn't a shyster, and Franson wouldn't have had his career enhanced by his death," Deacon said to Weber.

"I realize that, Deacon, but tell that to the Feds. They talk, and the chief jumps. I'll see what I can do." He turned and went back to his office up front.

Deacon looked over to me and smiled. "Screw it, I think I'll take the day off and go visit my wife and daughter. You with me?"

"I'm right there. Shall we go?"

We left the precinct in my car, and I drove Deacon to the hospital. He needed the rest after his blood pressure probably went through the roof. We arrived and went to the room where we found Lynn resting with Earl's girlfriend Paula holding the baby. She smiled and shushed us.

Deacon quietly went to her as she carefully held the baby up for him to take. I went to the side of the bed, took Lynn's hand and leaned over to give her a kiss on her forehead.

"Thanks for coming, Jim. Penny said she'd be back to visit today. I've been lonely this morning until Paula showed up."

"Well, we don't want to overwhelm you," I said.

"I can handle overwhelm. Now, how is the case going?"

I filled her in as Deacon was cooing his daughter on the couch across from Lynn's bed.

"The Feds took him, and Weber let them?" she said.

"They went over his head to the chief. He wasn't happy either."

"He'll be less happy when the mayor starts to bother him."

"I hope he tells the mayor to talk to the Feds. Franson wouldn't have had his career advanced by the Fed lawyer's death. Totally unrelated."

"Is that your professional opinion?" Lynn asked with a smile. Then she said more quietly, "How's Deacon doing?"

I leaned towards her and said, "He's doing fine, but I know he misses you. On the case, I mean. He has a low opinion of his abilities."

"I have to boost him up frequently. He's a good detective, but he has, as you said, a low opinion of his abilities. I don't know what to do about it. I usually just let him help me and he's happy."

"Yes, he likes letting you take the lead. I hope it's only on the job," I said with a grin.

"Jim, are you saying Deacon isn't manly in his husbandly duties?"

I didn't say anything, just smiled.

"Never fear, he's a tiger on the home front. He enjoys being married and having our home life as it is. I'm hoping he will take to having the baby around. He's going to have to change his macho attitude to be able to change diapers." She laughed and looked over to Deacon. "He's all I could ever want. Besides the baby."

We all sat around playing with the baby until Penny walked in. "Well, who's guarding Las Vegas?" she asked, seeing Deacon and me sitting on the couch with the baby.

"Las Vegas has agreed to stop having crime until we are done here," Deacon said.

Penny went to Lynn and said, "Have they told you when you'll be out of here?"

"They hope tomorrow. I'm doing well now, and I'm threatening to shoot them if I don't get out. They are trying to work on that."

"Jim and I will take the baby, as I said, and Jim is paying for your evening out with Deacon. A fine dinner at Momma Mia's and then a show, your choice."

"Oh, that sounds great, thanks. I just need to get out of here."

Deacon's cell phone buzzed, and he handed the baby to Paula. He answered and listened then hung up and turned to me. "We have to go."

He stood and went to Lynn, giving her a big kiss. "I'll be back later to tuck you in."

"Hell, I'm already tucked in. It would be nice to be untucked." She pulled him down and gave him a lip lock.

Deacon signaled me to follow, and we left the room. He went down the hallway with me tagging behind. He stopped at the elevators and pushed the button. "That was Warren on the phone. He did some digging around in bank accounts and came up with some interesting facts. Seems Franson has no big withdrawals in any account he had. Warren did a thorough search, and he had no other accounts. But the late Mr. Reese had three huge deposits on the day of each murder. Somehow Warren did a trace on the money transfer. Seems the money was moved from one account to Reese's. You'll never guess who made the money transfers."

*

Chapter 25

"Are you kidding me? I can't believe he would do that," I said. "How could he have himself killed in the hospital? He should have known that he might not have been brought back from being dead. I can see the gun shots at his home, he could have set that up himself, and the explosion. He hid in the closet behind tons of clothes so as not to be killed. But the attempted murder in the hospital still amazes me."

"I'll have CSI run his blood tests and see if he had one of those drugs that make it look like you're dead. Warren said Grisler transferred three payments to Reese's account since this all began, but none for his own attempts at murder. Why would he pay for his own death attempts when he could fake it?"

"Okay, I can see it now. Grisler comes to me with his story about someone wanting him murdered. I'll murder the creep myself now." I paused, thinking. "Then we take him to his house, leave him alone inside to set up the bomb, and he hides in the closet. We pull him out of the burning building, being the good guys we are, and take him to the hospital. Somehow he took some drug to simulate death. But who was the mysterious person leaving his room?"

"He could have had someone fake it. He paid someone to walk out at the right time. He's shrewd, he planned it carefully, and we were the patsies. I hope the Feds enjoy talking to Franson. I'm not telling anyone about this until we solve this."

We arrived at the hospital where Grisler was holed up. We went to his room and found it empty.

"What the hell!" Deacon bellowed. He turned to the cop standing in the hallway. "Where's Grisler?"

"They released him. Said he was okay to leave. I'm still here because I wasn't told to leave," the young cop said.

Deacon's face was turning red. "Okay! You can leave!" he yelled at the officer. "Leave, before I beat you to a pulp!"

The cop looked terrified and rushed off. Deacon turned to me and said, "This is not happening. We need to go to Grisler's office to see if he went there. He should have kept up the act and taken a cop with him." He yelled to the officer still waiting for the elevator, "You! Did Grisler leave alone or with someone?"

The officer jumped and said, "He took Granholm with him."

"Granholm? A cop?"

"Yes, sir. They told me to stay here." The officer looked confused. The elevator doors opened, but he made no move get on.

"Get the hell out!" Deacon yelled to him. The officer jumped into the elevator just before the doors closed.

"I don't know any Granholm." He pulled out his cell phone and made a call. "Warren, check to see if an officer Granholm was sent to guard Grisler. Call me back." He hung up and stood staring at the empty bed. "I'm not having a good day. This is so wrong. He can't go to his burnt out house, so let's go to his office and see if he's still playing the part."

We drove over to his office, but there was no one there. "I may have to put out an APB on him," Deacon said.

"If you do, the Feds may move in on him," I said.

"I'll make it look like he's wanted on a totally unrelated charge. Maybe we can get past the Feds. I'll talk to Warren and see what he can whip up for a warrant. He's the geek of this squad and can usually bypass most of our system."

"Okay, we need to find Grisler. Otherwise you have nothing else. Does he have any relatives in town?" I asked.

Deacon stared at me, frowned and then pulled out his cell phone. "Warren, can you check with someone who knows Grisler to see if he has any relatives in Vegas? Good, thanks. Oh, wait! Try to put out an APB on him but keep it on the down low so the Feds don't get wind of it. See if you can get an arrest warrant for Grisler, too. Good, thanks." Deacon hung up.

"Okay, it's set. Now we need to find the creep. All we can do now is wait." He sat back in the passenger seat and went quiet.

~~*~~

Trapper entered the Golden Shoe bar and, after his eyes adjusted to the flashing and strobe lights, he went to the first stage and sat. There was a brunette spinning around the pole in front of him. She stopped and slithered over to him, bringing her legs up, spreading for him.

He smiled and asked her if Peaches was dancing. The woman looked annoyed and said to go to hell. Trapper took it as a sign that Peaches was somewhere in the building. The waitress came over, and Trapper ordered a beer then asked her if Peaches was going to dance soon. The waitress said she would be out soon then scooted off.

Finally after two beers Peaches came out and up to the stage. She did her first dance without noticing Trapper. He just sat back and enjoyed the dance.

Her second dance started, and she threw off her top. It landed on Trapper. She spun around on the pole then went down to the stage floor and gyrated.

She looked over and saw Trapper. She smiled and rolled over to him.

"Hey, Mr. Trapper. Good to see you again." She spun on the floor a few times to the music and then spun back to him. She said, almost out of breath, "I got a visit from the detective in charge of Bobby's murder." Trapper clenched his teeth when he heard that. He had hoped Walt Hartley would back off Peaches now that he had fed Hartley the info about her alibi. "We had a long talk about the wife killing Bobby." She gyrated a little more and then jumped up to hit the pole one more time before the music ended.

Peaches came off the stage after the song finished and around to Trapper. She turned him in his chair and said, "I'll give you a free lap dance so I can talk to you. Walt said he got a call saying I was busy the night of Bobby's murder. Thanks for that." She was moving slowly on Trapper's lap. "He is such an interesting person for a cop. We talked on and off until the club closed, and then he took me for something to eat. We found a Coney place and had hot dogs. Funny name for food. I hope they don't make them from real dogs."

Trapper was getting distracted from her wiggling, trying to listen to what she was babbling about.

"Walt asked me to go out with him this weekend to see a new show over in the Krave Club. I think it's one of those sexy shows."

Now Trapper was not happy with his old enemy, Walt. "Are you going with him?" he asked.

"Oh, sure. It's good to have a cop with you when you go out at night. All those creeps out there, you know."

Yeah, you're going to be with one of those creeps, Trapper thought. The song ended and Peaches got up. "Did you come here to tell me something?"

Trapper thought for a moment then said. "No, nothing important. Hope your date goes well. I have to go, thanks for the dance." He stood, said good-bye to her and walked towards the door. Trapper hoped Hartley would choke on her G-string.

He was approaching his car as he pulled out his cell phone. He dialed Samantha, maybe to re-establish their relationship. At least Sam was not a bubblehead.

Deacon's cell buzzed and he answered. "Go ahead, Greg. Whatcha got?" He put it on speaker phone so I could hear.

"Grisler has a sister out in Spring Valley around Buffalo and Russell. I texted you the address. I got the APB and the warrant, so we got that covered. I did another check, and this morning Grisler withdrew the same amount as before from his account. He must have hired another hitman."

"Or paid the one who murdered Reese. Thanks, Greg. Let me know if you hear anything." He hung up.

"Okay, so Grisler is still paying off someone. I'm sure he doesn't know that we suspect him, so maybe he's not running. Yet. Let's go visit the sister. I hope she's not as evil as he is."

*

Chapter 26

We arrived at the house from the address Warren sent us. It was an older ranch style home, one story with desert landscaping. The valley was low on water so the city encouraged people to get rid of the grass and do the stone and cactus landscaping. There was one car in the driveway. An old beat up Chevy

Nova from around 1974, I'd say. Only because I had one just like it back then.

We exited my car and went up to the porch. Deacon knocked on the inner wooden door that was missing the outer screen door. We waited until we could hear movement. Then the door opened and there was a girl of about sixteen or so looking out at us.

"Yeah, what do you cops want?" she asked with a slight growl.

"We are looking for Alphonse Grisler. Would he be here?"

"Nope, Uncle Al doesn't like us. We're not his kind of people," she replied.

"What kind of people is that?" Deacon asked.

"Classy, rich people. We be the poor black sheep of the family. What do you want him for? Did he commit a crime, and you'll put him in prison?"

Apparently even his family hated the man. She looked back and forth at us as Deacon said, "We just want to talk to him. Has he been here recently?"

"He came by this morning and talked to Mom, then he left. I didn't ask where to, I didn't care."

“If you see him again, tell him to call me,” Deacon said, handing her his card. “Thanks. Oh, and where is your mother?”

“Don’t know, don’t care. Okay, I think I heard her say she was going to her bank.”

“How long ago?”

“Half hour, I guess.”

“What bank?”

“You ask a lot of questions.”

“It’s my job. Now what bank?”

“Bank of America over on Maryland.”

“Thank you. Have your uncle call me,” Deacon said, and we stepped off the porch as the girl shut the door.

“Nice family,” I said.

“If you like the Addams family.” Deacon smiled and we got back in the car.

“So, are we going to the bank?” I asked.

“If you don’t mind driving by. Do you know where it’s at?”

"Of course. I used to bank there when I first lived here. I didn't like them."

"Well, we just want to see if the sister is doing a deposit or withdrawal."

Deacon looked at the text on his phone and said, "Her name is Sybil McCroy. I hope the bank is cooperative in giving us the info."

"I doubt it, they aren't very friendly," I replied.

We drove over to Maryland and into the parking lot. The bank was near UNLV campus so there were a number of young people walking around carrying book bags. The area was a restaurant row with a number of fast food places. I looked across the street to the Carl's Jr. building and thought I'd mention stopping, but I'd wait until we found out anything in the bank.

We went in and Deacon flashed his badge then asked the guard for the manager. He indicated a woman in her 50s, dressed very businesslike. We went over to her desk.

"Excuse me. I was told you are the manager?" Deacon asked.

She looked carefully at Deacon's badge, like maybe others had come in with fake badges. "Yes, detective, what can I do for you?"

"We're investigating a series of murders. You may have heard about them on the news. All the lawyers."

"Yes, I have read about them. Tragic. What does this have to do with my bank?"

"Our main suspect has a sister who banks here, and we were wondering if we could find out if she has deposited or withdrawn any large amounts of cash within the last day or two."

"Well, detective, do you have a warrant?"

"Uh, no. But I'm hoping you can give us something without breaking any bank rules or laws." Deacon gave her a big smile.

She hesitated then said, "What is her name?"

"Sybil McCroy. Not a common name."

The woman went to a terminal and did some typing. She waited then said, "I'm not telling you this, but that woman made a rather large deposit just today. That's all I can give you."

"Large, as in over five thousand dollars?" he asked, knowing what Grisler had transferred to Reese's account.

She didn't say a word, just nodded slightly and said, "If that's all you need, I have to get back to work."

"Thank you so much for your time." Deacon turned to me and motioned to go.

Outside, I asked, "What does that prove?"

"I don't know for sure, but maybe Grisler's sister is going to hire someone and he gave her the cash to do it."

"That's reasonable. Now where to?"

Deacon looked across the street at the fast food places. "Shall we grab a quick bite to eat while we wait for Grisler to be spotted?"

We stopped in at Carl's Jr. and had our burgers and fries. "I've heard about the 5 Guys burgers and fries. Have you ever eaten there?" I asked.

"No, but I've heard they have good burgers. There's one down at the Vegas Outlet Center. We'll have to try it sometime."

We finished our burgers and went back to the car. "I don't know where to go, do you?"

Deacon pulled out his cell phone and made a call. "Warren, anything on Grisler?" He listened then said, "We just went to his sister's bank and they said she made a big deposit. Check on her financials and see what she may be up to. Talk later." He hung up and said, "Nothing on Grisler yet. Maybe he went to the courthouse to check on his dockets. It's someplace to go at least."

I started the Crown Vic and drove to the courthouse. We went in to the security checkpoint, and Deacon badged the deputy at the metal detectors. He cleared me through, and we went to the office for court cases. Deacon went up to the clerk and showed his badge. I should mention to him to get one of those badges that hung from around his neck so he wasn't wearing his pants pocket out.

"Hi, can you tell me if Alphonse Grisler has checked in on any of his cases?" he asked her.

She thumbed through her books and said, "No, he hasn't been around for a few days. Sorry."

We left the courthouse feeling depressed. Grisler was out there somewhere, but we didn't know where. We sat in the car, and Deacon's cell buzzed again.

"Yeah, Greg," he answered and put the phone on speaker.

"Granholm doesn't exist anywhere in the system. I talked to Baker, the cop you frightened half to death at the hospital. He said that this Granholm came in and told the one cop he could go back to duty. Baker didn't question the guy, he had on the whole uniform. Grisler called for a doctor and insisted that he wanted out, so the doctor released him. Baker said they told him to stay in case anyone came looking for them. He did, and Grisler left with the fake cop. I'm surprised that Grisler didn't figure that we'd catch on."

"Maybe Grisler isn't doing this to get ahead in the gene pool, or I should say lawyer pool. Maybe he's planning on skipping after he kills off his enemies," I said.

Deacon agreed. "Greg, have our guys watch McCarron Airport in case he decides to take a trip. Just for the hell of it, cover our bases. Find out anything on the sister?"

"Yeah, she's suddenly rich. About a hundred grand in her bank account as of today. Grisler's account is now down by about a hundred grand. I think he may be hiding his money. If he takes a trip it would be harder for us to watch his money trail. But now that we know his sister has it, we can still track him."

"Good work, Greg. Call me if anything pops." He hung up and sat back in the seat. "I'm feeling like Grisler may be heading out."

"Why would he go to all this trouble to take the heat off him by being part of the murders? He must have planned on hanging around to enjoy the lack of competition," I said.

"Unless he found out we were on to him. He has connections, I'm sure he's been watching our moves."

I was watching the people come and go into the courthouse, wondering what crimes they committed that some lawyer would get them off.

"I wonder what ever happened to the divorce case Grisler had me testifying for? Did they postpone it when Grisler went missing? He would have had someone to back up on the case if he couldn't finish," I said.

"Interesting. Maybe that lawyer would know Grisler's habits and where he might be. Let's go back in and see who it was," Deacon said as he opened the car door.

We went back to the clerk who checked her books and found that the case continued with another lawyer, Nick Seely. Deacon asked if he was in the building. The clerk said he had a case going on in small claims. She gave us the directions and Deacon thanked her.

"I'm hoping this will give us something," he said looking more depressed.

*

Chapter 27

We headed up to the small claims court, taking the stairs to get some exercise. We found one of the court officers whom Deacon knew.

"Hey, Max, how are you doing?" Deacon asked the man who was almost bigger than Deacon.

"Good, Deacon. I hear you're a daddy now."

"Yep, baby girl, looks like her mother," Deacon replied.

"Thankfully for her. What are you doing in small claims? Bragging about your virility?"

"Haha. I need to know who and where is Nick Seely?"

"Oh, the junior Grisler. He's in the second room on the right. If you could take him with you, we'd all appreciate it."

"I'm not taking any lawyer, except to jail. You haven't seen Grisler by chance?"

"Sure, he came through here to talk to his protégé," Max said.

Deacon suddenly came to life. "When? Where did he go?"

"About an hour ago, don't know where he went to."

"Crap, did you hear anything they said?"

"Nope, they talked quietly, then Grisler left. Seely went back into the courtroom. He's still in there."

"How would you like to help me arrest Seely?"

"Can I beat him?" he asked.

"Whatever. Is this case ending soon, or do we go in and take him?"

"I'll look," the big man said and went into the courtroom.

"See, things may work out yet," I said as Deacon looked like he might explode.

"Jim, this may be the break we've been waiting for. If this Seely talked to Grisler, he has to know something about Grisler's plans. If this guy doesn't talk I may have to beat it out of him." Deacon was starting to pace. "What's taking Max so long?"

"He's only been gone a few minutes. He can't interrupt the court. Give it time," I said, hoping Deacon would calm down. I'd never seen him so strung out. I think the stress of the baby and Lynn being gone was having an effect on him.

The door to the courtroom opened and Max came back out. "Couple more minutes, they're almost done. I told him there was someone who wanted to talk to him about a case. He sure looked like he wanted another case. I didn't mention you were the police."

"Good, I don't want him skipping out either. I've had enough of that. Was Grisler alone when he came in?"

"No, some guy was with him. Big guy, reminded me of a cop. But I don't think he was."

"Can I get a copy from the security cameras on this floor?"

"Sure, I'll call them and explain. They can make a copy while you wait." He pulled out his cell phone and went to a corner for privacy.

Deacon and I stood waiting until Max came back and told us they'd get a copy out to us. They knew who to look for. Grisler was well known around this building, which surprised me. Since he was so well known, why did he come into the building? Wasn't he worried that someone would see him? I was going to give up trying to figure out Grisler's thought process.

The door to the courtroom opened again and four people came out. They were arguing about some property they owned and didn't want to give up. One man, who I presumed was Seely, was trying to calm them.

"I'll file an appeal and we'll get your land back to you, don't you worry," he said.

"You better or I'm going to take a piece of your land. Your ass!" one of the men told Seely. Then three of the men stormed off. Seely turned to us and asked if we wanted to speak to him.

"Mr. Seely, I'm Detective DeAngelo, and you are coming with us to my precinct to talk about Alphonse Grisler. Please follow me."

Seely got a wide-eyed look and started to turn to run, but Max was behind him and grabbed him by the throat. He held him in place while Deacon handcuffed him.

"You just had to run, now you go down under arrest. Thanks, Max." Deacon turned to me and said, "We can't take him in your car. I'll grab a couple uniforms downstairs to haul him in. Let's go, Seely."

He started protesting, and Deacon told him to shut up until they got to the precinct. Then he could yell all he wanted.

On the main floor of the courthouse, Deacon found a couple officers doing nothing and had them take Seely in. We went to my car and followed the cop car.

I parked in the back and we went in as the cops were putting Seely in an interrogation room. They handcuffed him to the table and left. Deacon thanked them and went in. I went to observation.

"Mr. Seely, you just had to make it hard on yourself by trying to run. Dumb move. I only wanted to talk to you about your partner Grisler. From an eyewitness, Grisler was seen today talking to you in the courthouse. What did he want?"

"That's privileged information," Seely said.

"Grisler isn't your client, privilege doesn't count. What did Grisler talk to you about?"

Seely went silent. Deacon leaned over to him and said, "Look, Seely, we are going to arrest Grisler for conspiracy to commit murder. You know, the three lawyers who were murdered this week. Grisler did that. Now if you don't cooperate, I'll have the charges include you for being an accessory to murder. That will bring your law career to a screeching halt. Now tell me what Grisler is up to."

Seely looked like he was considering his options. "If I cooperate, I'll not be included in this?"

"You'll just be a material witness. Now what did Grisler talk to you about?"

"He asked me to take his cases for a couple days. He said he was going out of town to get away from the killings of the lawyers. He didn't say he did it. Just that he wanted to protect himself."

"Who was the man with him?"

"Grisler introduced him as a bodyguard. He said the man's name was Jason Griggs."

Deacon wrote the name on the notepad he took from his pocket. He stood and went to the door calling for Warren. Warren came over and Deacon said something to him then gave him the slip of paper. I figured he was going to have Greg check on the man. Deacon went back to the table and sat.

"How long have you known Grisler?"

"A couple years. I tolerated him the first year until I learned his tricks for being an ass. I put up with him since. I wouldn't put it past him to have those men killed. Grisler always bitched about how they were taking the good cases from him. Grisler was also bucking to be elected as District Attorney. He was going to start his campaign in a month or two. I can see why he wanted those men out of the way. They all had an eye on the job, too." Seely was loosening up now.

"Did Grisler say where he was going for the few days?"

"He mentioned Reno. But I know he hated the city. He was a lawyer there for a couple years but they gave him a hard time. Most of the other lawyers didn't like him. He moved here because there were more lawyers and he could hide in the numbers. He hired me to do his dirty work, take the cases he didn't want to handle. I've been putting up with him until I can go out on my own."

Warren tapped on the door window. Deacon stood and went over there. Warren said something to him, then Deacon closed the door and returned to Seely.

"Seems your partner has been consorting with criminals. I'm surprised that Griggs used his real name. Seems he is a convicted murderer, served ten years and is out on parole. The jails just can't hold all the murderers they have. We have a warrant out on him now, too, so if you can tell me anything more it will be a feather in your bonnet."

Seely was frowning. "I don't know much more I can tell you. All Grisler said was to take his cases and he was going to be out of town for a short while. He didn't even say how long. I asked, and he said he wasn't sure. This doesn't make sense. Grisler had plans to get elected and then he'd have the power to rule the DA's office. From what you say, he's screwed."

Deacon stood up and said, "Yes, he is screwed. Okay, I'll have a car take you back to the courthouse. Don't you leave town either."

He turned and left the room. I came out of observation and said, "You're turning him loose?"

Deacon signaled to Warren. "Have a couple detectives on Seely's ass to watch where he goes." He turned to me. "Yes, I'm cutting him loose. Maybe he'll lead us to Grisler."

*

Chapter 28

We watched as an officer led Seely out of the precinct. Warren told Deacon that he had Williams and another detective waiting outside to follow Seely from the courthouse. Deacon said to keep him informed.

"Why don't we follow him?" I asked.

"He knows me now, and he saw you with me at the courthouse. He'd spot us in a minute. Williams may be a screw up but he is good at tracking. He'll report in on what he finds. Shall we go to the iron kitchen and wait?"

We went to the new breakroom that the precinct had built taking over for the one that shared the storeroom. It was nice. New machines for coffee, pop and snacks. There was even one machine that had sandwiches in it.

I was standing looking in at a tuna on wheat and said, "How often do they change these?"

"They come in every morning. The machine is usually empty by four. That sandwich should be fresh," he said as he pulled a knob for a Reese's Peanut Butter Cup on the next machine.

We sat on the nice new tables and chairs. "They spared no expense building this room. Although I kind of miss the storeroom atmosphere," Deacon said with a laugh.

"So Grisler plans to kill the lawyers after implicating himself as a victim to throw us off. Did he really think it wise to pay the killer with funds from his own bank account? That wasn't smart," I said.

"No one said Grisler was smart. He's a weasel who wants to get ahead any way he can. I suppose he really believed he could get away with it."

"Well, I hope he gets a lawyer just like him. That would be punishment enough," I said.

"Maybe Seely could take the case." Deacon laughed. "No, I think Seely would rather he rot in jail."

"I think we all would like him to rot in jail."

Deacon's cell phone buzzed and he looked at it. "Williams already," he said with a half puzzled look. "That was quick." He put it on speaker then answered, "Whatcha you got, Williams?"

"The patrol car dropped him in front of the courthouse. He didn't go in, just headed to the parking lot and got in a car. His, according to the license plates. We followed him out, and now we are on Charleston just past Decatur heading west. I'll let you know where he goes from here."

"Great, we'll head to Charleston to follow. Keep me apprised of the situation." He hung up.

"Apprised? Still using the word book I see," I said, trying not to laugh.

"Shut up and follow if you want to go." He stood and headed back outside, this time to his unmarked car. He started the car, grabbed the radio mic and called for Williams. Williams replied.

"What's your ten-twenty?" Deacon asked.

"We just moved past Decatur. There was an accident that held us up. We're still heading west on Charleston."

"I'm coming out. Keep the line open and let me know what he's up to."

"Acknowledged," Williams said.

Deacon put on the sirens and flashers to get us up to Charleston. He avoided the strip and took Tropicana out to Decatur then up towards Charleston. I had only been in a car once with Deacon driving using the full police mode. He's a scary driver. I think if it was allowed he'd use the sidewalks.

It was a long trip up Decatur, and the road turned into divided highways a couple times. We got to Charleston and turned left across the divided highway, I'm sure scaring a few drivers. We were now on Charleston heading West.

Deacon called Williams again to find out their location.

"We're heading North on Rainbow, just past Summerlin Parkway. I think he's turning west on Lake Mead Boulevard," Williams said.

"He's in Summerlin. Why would he go there? Not to the federal lawyer's house, I'm sure," I said.

"It's still a crime scene. He shouldn't be going there. I don't know where Seely lives. Call Warren and see," Deacon requested.

I pulled out my cell phone and hit the speed dial for Warren. He came on quickly, and I asked him to find out where Seely lived. I could hear him typing on the keyboard and then he told me. I thanked him and hung up.

"Seely does live in Summerlin. On Coral Shores Drive. Warren is texting you the address," I said.

Deacon reached in his coat for his cell phone and checked the messaging. He reached for the mic again and called Williams to give him the address.

Williams' voice came back out of the radio. "I know. He just pulled up to the house. We're holding back for now until you get here."

"We should be there in a few minutes." He clicked off the mic and turned off the sirens. "No sense in giving Seely an advance warning. The Summerlin LVPD precinct is about a half mile from where Seely lives. We should give them a courtesy call that we are going to raid their neighborhood."

He got on the radio again and called Williams to have him contact the Summerlin LVPD. He said he would.

"You know we have no cause to bust in on Seely. All we know is he's going home. Probably to change his underwear from you scaring him," I said.

Deacon laughed. "Yeah, that's true. We'll just give him a friendly visit and go from there."

We arrived on the street and pulled up behind Williams. An unmarked LVPD car pulled up behind us. A very big black man in a dark suit got out and came to Deacon who was exiting our car.

"DeAngelo! They let you go out on cases?" the big man said.

"Yes, Charles, they do. Have you caught the killer of your federal lawyer yet?"

"Hell, no. The Feds won't let us even near the place now. Whatcha got going here?"

Deacon explained what we were up to as I came around the car. Deacon introduced me to Charles Newcome, detective. The big man shook my hand, nearly crushing it. I hated it when people didn't think about how much strength they exerted on somebody else's hand.

"Good to meet you, Richards." He smiled and turned to Deacon. "So I'll hang back and let you run this. I'm sure you'll need me to watch your back." He laughed.

"I don't trust you with my back, Chuck. You probably have a knife in your pocket."

"Hey, all us brothers carry knives. It's part of the code." He laughed.

"Yeah, right. Okay, let's see what we got here." Deacon turned his attention to the house about half way down the block. There was one car in the drive and one at the curb. Williams had already run the plate on the car at the curb and said it belonged to Jason Griggs.

"Well, that settles it. Grisler has to be in there. Seely was part of this." He paused then said, "Chuck, can you get some backup here?"

"Hell, Summerlin is such a quiet place, my men are just sitting around waiting for some action." He went to his car and got on his radio.

We watched the house. Nothing was going on. About five minutes later four patrol cars came screeching down the road from both ways and stopped by the house. Deacon and Williams ran up to the front door, and Deacon banged, standing off to the side. I stood back by the sidewalk with Newcome.

"Seely, it's the police, open up," Deacon yelled to the door. They waited until there was a barrage of gunfire zipping through the door.

Newcome and I both took a dive behind a car as the rounds of ammo whizzed past us. All of Newcome's men went on alert and surrounded the house. Deacon waited, then kicked in the door, and the armor plated officers poured in.

I didn't hear any more gun fire, so I came around the car and up cautiously to the house.

I could hear men shouting clear, then it started again. It sounded like the fourth of July with gun fire echoing out the front door. Then it got quiet again.

An officer came out and yelled to Newcome to get a bus, referring to an ambulance. He got on his radio and made a call.

I started to worry that the bus was for Deacon. I said the hell with it and went in the house. The cops were all over the place. Suddenly two of them appeared, escorting Seely out in cuffs. I yelled to Williams who was at the top of stairs going up to the second floor.

"Is Deacon all right?" I called to him.

"I'm fine, Jim," Deacon said, coming around a corner. "Griggs is dead, but Grisler's not here."

*

Chapter 29

"Did Seely say anything about Grisler's whereabouts?" I asked.

"All he said was, screw you, and then he shut up. I felt like shooting him in the nuts and saying he was hit during the gunfight, but there were too many witnesses." He smiled and we went out of the house.

"Now we're back to square one. Trying to find Grisler."

"Unless he has another house somewhere, maybe he's hiding out at his office? Griggs had to have dropped him somewhere and his office has all his paperwork about his cases. Maybe he needed something?"

"We can swing by there just to satisfy you. Okay?"

"It'll make my day," I said.

Deacon told Williams to handle the situation there as we were going to see if we could still track down Grisler. Deacon said good-bye to Newcome, and we went to the car. Deacon stopped on the passenger side and said, "Crap."

I looked over to where he was looking and saw the back tire was flat. Must have been hit by a stray bullet. Deacon went back to Williams, took the keys to his car and said they were trading. Of course, Williams didn't know the tire was flat.

"He deserves the exercise," Deacon said with a laugh.

We left the area and drove to Grisler's office. "Is there going to be anyone there?" I asked. "Other than Grisler?"

"If you were such a great detective, you would have noticed the name on the door, Grisler and Osterman, Attorneys at Law. He had another lawyer sharing the space."

"Sounds like Grisler, cheap."

We arrived and went into the building. The same secretary was at the desk and smiled when we came up. "Good afternoon, officers. How is Mr. Grisler feeling today?" She didn't know he was our suspect now.

"He's missing. We're trying to locate him before he gets hurt."

The woman looked shocked. "How did he go missing?"

"He left the hospital without us knowing, and we can't find him. You wouldn't by chance have heard from him today?"

"No, I figured he was still in the hospital. His house is totaled so he couldn't go there. He could have gone to his girlfriend's house."

Deacon smiled and asked, "Who is this girlfriend? And where do we find her?"

The woman went through her rolodex and pulled a card. She wrote something on a slip of paper and gave it to Deacon. “Amber Holloway. She’s a court reporter and quite cute. If there's anywhere Mr. Grisler would go, it would be there.” Deacon thanked her.

I looked around the room and saw a couple posters leaning against the wall. They had promotions for Osterman running for DA. It struck me funny that Grisler didn’t have any posters.

“Why doesn’t Grisler have any posters for his campaign to run for DA?” I asked the woman.

“Mr. Grisler wasn’t going to run. He knew he couldn’t win with his reputation.”

I looked at Deacon and he had that look on his face. I said to him, “Seely lied about Grisler running.”

“Yeah, Grisler would have had no reason to murder his competition if he had no competition. We need to talk to Seely.” Deacon thanked the woman and we left.

In the car Deacon said, “We’ll swing by this Amber person's place and see if Grisler is holed up there.” He started the car and drove out.

We arrived at the house and there was a fairly attractive woman out front trimming the bushes. We approached as she wiped sweat from her brow with a cloth. "Can I help you gentlemen?" she asked.

"Are you Amber Holloway?"

"I am, and you are?"

"Detective DeAngelo, and this is Jim Richards, consultant to the LVMPD. Can you tell us if you have seen Alphonse Grisler?"

"I haven't seen him and don't want to see him."

"Oh, aren't you his girlfriend?"

"Was. He has too much baggage and I don't appreciate his threats. Sorry, I should say, his partner's threats."

"Which partner would that be?"

"That Jason person, I don't remember his last name."

"Griggs?"

"Yeah, that sounds like it. He said that I was to not see Grisler ever again. If Al couldn't tell me himself, I don't want anything to do with him."

“This Griggs told you that alone, without Grisler?”

“Yeah, he said Al was busy.”

“When was this?”

“Yesterday. It was late in the day. If Al is in trouble, he deserves it. His gambling was going to catch up with him sooner or later.”

“Gambling. Grisler gambles?” I asked.

“No, he loses. And the people he borrows money from aren’t happy with him. Grigg worked for one of the bookies. I took it as a sign that Al didn’t want to see me anymore. Fine with me. He’s a toad anyway.”

Deacon asked, “You wouldn’t know where he may be?”

“At his house I would imagine.”

“You didn’t hear? His house was blown up. Grisler’s been in the hospital for a few days.”

She looked a little shocked and said, “I didn’t know. Why didn’t Griggs say something?”

"I guess he wanted you to stay away. Sorry to have troubled you. Thanks," Deacon said, and we went back to the car.

"Something ain't right here," Deacon said. "Grisler is becoming a mystery now. He's not running for office, he has a gambling problem, and Griggs works for a bookie. I'm getting bad signals here. What does this have to do with the death of the lawyers?"

"Maybe the murdered lawyers were the bookies." I laughed. "Grisler murdered them to get out of his debts."

"You know, that's not too far from the truth. When I was on vice, we did a bust on a lawyer who fronted a bookie operation. I'll call a friend in Vice and see what he knows. If Griggs worked for a bookie, maybe he was in on cutting out the competition, too."

"I can see if Trapper can talk to Sam to see what she may know," I said.

"First, we need to talk to Seely. Shall we go?"

We went back to the precinct, and Deacon went into interrogation. I sat in observation watching Seely sitting quietly. Deacon sat across from him and said, "Seely, we have a lot of facts about your buddy Grisler. He's a gambler, owes a lot of money. Were the lawyers who were murdered involved in gambling?"

Deacon waited for Seely to say something. He just stared at the table, saying nothing.

"Come on, Seely, talk to me." He didn't. "Are you going to sit there and implicate yourself in these crimes?"

He still said nothing. Then he said, "I want my lawyer."

Deacon shook his head and stood. "Okay Seely, play this game. We'll find Grisler without you, and you two can share a cell." Deacon left the room. I went out and met him in the squad room.

"He's not going to talk, even with a lawyer. I think he's frightened about something. I'm wondering if Grisler is pulling the strings or someone else."

"We've got Seely, Griggs is dead, we can rest on Grisler for now. He won't be killing anyone else now that we know he's behind it."

"True. I think I'll let Seely stew in holding for the night again. He didn't learn the last time. I think I may want to go see my family now. I'm tired of all this."

"I'm sure Penny would like to see me, too. Shall we leave this nut house?" I said just as my cell phone buzzed. I looked at the caller ID and it read, Penny. "Hey, babe, what's up?"

"Nothing much, lover," came a male voice from my phone. I tensed and grabbed Deacon's arm. He gave me a strange look as he saw my face scrunch up.

"Who is this?" I asked.

"Oh, come on, Richards. I'm your client. You still haven't found out who was trying to kill me." It was Grisler. And he had Penny's phone.

"What do you want, Grisler? If you hurt my wife, I'll be the one who wants to kill you. And I will."

"Oh, Richards, you can't kill anyone. You're too nice of a person."

"I killed the first man who threatened my wife. I have killed, and I will do it again. You want to talk, fine, let my wife go."

"Oh no, she's my ticket out. Is your buddy DeAngelo there? You two are always together."

"He's here. What do you want?"

"I just want you to listen, closely."

*

Chapter 30

"Okay, Grisler, I'm listening. What do you want?" I said as Deacon leaned toward me to hear better. I put the phone on speaker so he could hear.

"Hello, detective, I could hear the phone go to speaker. How are you doing today?" Grisler said smoothly.

"Screw you, Grisler. What do you want? Let's get this over with so I can put you behind bars," Deacon spit back.

"Now, now, DeAngelo. That's not the attitude. You need to be nice if you want to see Richards' wife alive again. Isn't she your daughter's namesake?"

"Don't you even talk about my daughter, you scum! You're not worthy to talk about her!" I pushed Deacon back a little. He was getting too close to my phone. He looked madder than I had seen him earlier.

"Okay, Grisler, let's talk nice now. What is it you want?" I said.

"What else? Safe passage out of Vegas. Maybe South America? Any country that doesn't have extradition. Look that up in your Google. I'll leave it to you where I go. Just make it nice and sunny."

In the background I heard Penny yell, "Don't listen to him. We're at the house."

I heard a gunshot, and my body chilled. I screamed into the phone, "Grisler, you are dead if she is hurt!!"

"Oh, come on, Bubby, I wouldn't hurt her. I need her safe and sound to make my getaway. I just frightened her a little. Oh, you need to fix the hole in your wall. Now get me out of here. Helicopter, train, plane, whatever it takes to move me to safety." The phone clicked off.

Deacon was on the phone calling for cars to go my house. I was worried that would be bad for Penny. But it needed to be done. Deacon finished and called to everyone in the squad explaining the situation. We ran to our car and drove to my home followed by every cop who wasn't doing anything.

We arrived and there were about seven patrol cars and one SWAT van parked out front. It looked like an attack on a drug house. Deacon came up to the SWAT leader and explained the situation.

My cell phone rang again. It was from Penny's phone. I answered.

"Not very smart, Richards. Now your wife is going to suffer," he said.

"So are you, Grisler. You know that you aren't going to get away alive now. If my wife is hurt, I'll be the one shooting you."

"Let's talk this out. You don't want your wife hurt. I don't want to die. What say I just take her out in one of your cars and drive away. I'll drop her off out in the desert and drive away. We both win."

"Yeah, drop her off in the desert, alive or dead?"

"Richards, alive, of course."

"Grisler, while we are waiting for your execution, why don't you explain how this mess started?"

There was a long pause, then he said, "Okay, it can't hurt now." I put the phone on speaker. "Okay, now that everyone is listening, I'll explain."

The man was so egotistical, he was confessing. I had a call recorder on my phone and turned it on.

"I had gambling problems. Griggs came to collect and liked the setup with my law firm. He talked to his boss, and they made an agreement to force me to take down the other lawyers. Those lawyers were involved with a mob in New Jersey and in local gambling. If they were gone, the link to the Jersey mob would lose their hold here, and Griggs' boss would take over."

"Who's that local boss?"

"Sweet Bennie. I don't suppose you know him?"

I knew Trapper's father was a friend of Sweet Bennie, as he was called. Trapper would not be happy. "I know who he is. What more is there?"

"I hired Reese to take them out, and I made it look like I was part of the attack. Reese got cocky and wanted more money, so Griggs took him out. If you can't figure out the rest you need to retire, old man."

I heard a barking in the background. It was Willy. The barking got louder and then I heard another gun shot. The men outside jumped when they heard that. I was afraid they'd go in shooting.

"Grisler, what happened? What did you do?"

There was no sound, Grisler didn't answer. Then I heard a familiar voice on the phone. It was Penny.

"Sweetie, you can come in. Grisler's down for the count," she said.

I slid the phone into my pocket and ran to the house followed by the SWAT team. I burst through the door with guns all around me.

Penny was standing in the living room holding the phone in one hand and the fire extinguisher in her arms. Grisler was on the floor. I came over to her and threw my arms around her. Willy bounced around our feet.

"What the hell happened?" I asked.

"Grisler was walking around the room bragging on the phone. Willy must have woke up. He came in from the bedroom and started barking. Grisler turned his back to me to fire his gun at Willy, but he missed. I picked up the fire extinguisher that you put on the table when Grisler first came in the house and hit him with it. Glad you didn't put it away." She looked down at Grisler. "Son of a bitch."

The cops gathered up Grisler, and Deacon congratulated Penny.

I smiled at my wonder woman. "You are amazing. Do you think you are getting used to be held by criminals?"

"Oh, actually, I'm getting tired of it. Can you go into another profession?" she said with a smile.

"You wouldn't be happy if you couldn't shoot someone or hit someone on the head with a pipe or fire extinguisher."

"Actually, that's true. It has been a fun ride. But seriously, can we take a vacation? Get away from all this for a while?"

"I think it can be arranged," I said.

The house had been cleared and we sat on the couch with Willy on my lap.

We had a good number of beers sitting in a cooler next to the couch. We were celebrating the end of the case.

"No more cases for lawyers, please," she whispered in my ear.

"No more cases at all for a while. I'll talk to Earl and Trapper and tell them to take the firm over. We need a rest. How's that sound?"

“Wonderful. We can take the van and live like vagabonds on the road.”

I smiled at her and put my head on her shoulder. Willy gave us a big sigh.

~~*~~

EPILOGUE

With Grisler incarcerated, Seely was spilling his guts. Seems he was dragged into the scheme to cover for Grisler while he was hiding from his fake murderer. Then Seely let Grisler use his house to keep from being caught by the police. He was given a lie to tell if asked and he went along with it. He’d do some time for aiding in a criminal operation.

Grisler told the judge during his arraignment that he was going to handle his own case. The judge didn’t argue, he knew Grisler was a lousy lawyer and would probably get himself put away for a long time. We all agreed.

Sweet Bennie’s bookie operation was shut down and he was charged with conspiracy to commit murder. Trapper wasn’t happy with his father’s friend, but Bennie went along with the plot, so he’d have to do some time. If he lived, Bennie was in his late eighties.

I talked to Lacey, Earl, Trapper and Buck about Penny and me skipping out of town for a while. That pleased everyone. Which bothered me a little.

Penny took the time off before her new network show would start. They delayed production for two weeks. That gave the network more time to promote her coming back.

We packed a number of things we would need to survive and climbed into the van. Willy was seated on a little chair I made for him to sit between us. It even had a little seatbelt. Penny asked where we were heading.

"I think I'll just get on the freeway and go. We'll stop wherever we feel like it." I said.

Penny grinned and said, "Aye, Captain, warp speed 10, full ahead."

I smiled and said, "Make it so," and drove out to our new adventure.

THE END

For every ending, there's a new beginning

Here's a sneak-peek at the next book, "Campground Murders". This book is a cross over between my two series of books, the Jim Richards murder novels and my Fatal series books.

Chapter 1

We were one day out of Las Vegas on the road north. Penny and I had decided that we wanted to see Seattle and climb the space needle. We had two weeks to travel out and then back to Vegas for Penny's show premiere. I figured that Seattle was close, yet far enough to enjoy the first week. Then down the coast to LA. My GPS was arguing with me most of the way up. I threw it in the back of the van and let Penny navigate.

"I think we should have turned right on that last road, Sweetie," she said.

"It would've been nice if you'd told me a little further in advance before I get us lost. There is no straight shot to Seattle from Vegas, and I'm not sure if we can make it up there and back in a week going this way. The main highway to the great Pacific

Northwest runs through California. This way is a mess of highways that go north, then south, then west. We can go a couple hundred miles out of the way to California, then up. This way will take forever."

"I'm looking at the map. This way will take us to Washington State if we jog over to Reno."

"Okay, how much longer?" I asked.

"She took out a small ruler to measure the scale of miles, then measured the map. "When we get to Reno, it's about 750 miles straight up." She was looking at her cell phone. It had the map information. "It should take us twelve and a half hours driving straight through."

"Are you serious? I'm not driving twelve and a half hours. You want to take over, fine. I'll do six hours, you take the rest. I've had enough of the Stratosphere in Vegas. Why do we have to climb the Space Needle? Are you going to push me off that structure so I can say I've been nearly killed twice from a half mile up?"

"Silly, no. The Space Needle is a historical landmark. It was made years ago for the Seattle World's Fair. You can jump if you want, but I won't push you."

"Thank you, that's comforting to know. I'm sure you'll want to go to the original Seattle Starbucks to get a cup of coffee?"

"Of course. I'm not fond of coffee, but I want to say I've tasted it from their first store."

"I'm sure it tastes the same as from the millionth store," I said.

"Where's your sense of adventure?" she asked.

"I left it back in Fallon. We should have stopped there for directions."

"You don't need directions; I'm going to get us there. See! There's a sign saying we are heading to Reno."

"Isn't Reno where people can get a quickie divorce?"

"Never mind. We're stuck with each other. No quickie divorces for us," she replied.

"What about that death do us part thing?"

"You go ahead and jump from the Space Needle if you really want that option." She smiled.

"Okay, we're stuck with each other. I'm a coward when it comes to killing myself."

Willy came up to the front of the van and barked. I looked down at him and said, "What? You have to go now?" I looked at Penny. "See, we should have stopped in Fallon."

"Fine, pull over and let the dog relieve himself. Better than stinking up the van."

I saw a small turnout in the road and pulled over. We all got out of the van and stretched our legs. Willy was put on a leash and we let him do his business.

"Does the air seem fresher out here? The air in Vegas is too dusty," I said.

"Sweetie, it sits in a desert. Of course there's more dust," Penny replied as she let the leash run out to its end. Willy scouted trees and then relieved himself.

"I can't watch the dog. It'll make me want to go, too," I said.

"You know where the toilet is. Just be sure to close the door. We are out in the public now."

"Nobody can see the toilet from outside. You just don't like looking at me on the toilet. It's good you have your own bathroom back home. You don't have to look at me taking a dump," I said with a grin.

“I may not see you but I can smell you,” she said then went around the van, pulled by Willy.

“Hey, my poop don’t stink,” I yelled to her on the other side of the van.

“So you think. Can we talk about something else?” she yelled back.

“Fine, is Willy done sniffing every bush?”

“He's digging now. Maybe he smells treasure.”

“Or a dead body,” I said quietly.

“Don’t you even mention dead bodies or murder at any time we are on this trip,” she said, coming up behind me from around the front of the van. Willy bounced at my feet. I bent down and picked him up.

“Yes, dear, I won’t mention it. You know it’s been nice that my cell phone hasn’t buzzed once since we left,” I said.

“It’s only been a day. Give Deacon time to start worrying about how to change a diaper,” she said as she unhooked the leash.

“I think Lynn can help him with that.”

She wound the leash and said, “You couldn’t change diapers, could you?”

“No, I have a very low threshold for bad smells. Can we talk about something other than poop?” I asked.

“Well, you brought it up. Twice. Now can we get moving? It’s going to get dark soon,” she said and went around the other side of the van to get in.

I looked at Willy in my arms and said, “Don’t ever get married.”

“I heard that!” came Penny’s voice from the van. I swear she had radar.

I got in, dropped Willy on the floor and started up the van. “See if there’s a campground or Walmart around Reno.”

“Walmart?” She gave me a strange look.

“Sure, Wally World. Most of the RV people know that Walmart is friendly to us resting in their parking lots. They’re smart. If we stop there for the night we will most likely buy something from them. They win, and we do, too.”

“I’m not camping out in a parking lot. I want a fire and marshmallows.” Penny pulled out her phone to look up campgrounds.

"I hate marshmallows," I said, turning up my nose.

"You hate everything," she replied.

"I like you."

"Don't start that again. We've been down this line of reasoning before. Okay, I found a nice small RV park on the Nevada and California border. Keep on this highway until we get to Reno then north on 395. I'll guide you there."

"Now I'm sure we will get lost."

"You can do this yourself and I'll drive," she said.

"No, dear, you're doing fine. Just get us there before midnight."

"Another hour, and it's still light out."

We drove on through Reno. I didn't want to visit. I'd heard it was congested with people. It's the little Las Vegas and spa city of north Nevada. You can gamble your money away and get divorced all in one setting. We journeyed out on Interstate 395 until we got close to Border Town. That, for obvious reasons, reminded me of the Mad Max movies. I was expecting to see a bunch of makeshift vehicles roaring out of the desert, shooting my tires out, then Mel Gibson coming to our rescue.

Penny was still consulting her maps and phone, guiding our vehicle to the RV Park. It turned out to be a small, rundown campground with about ten spaces for smaller RVs. I pulled up to a house and got out. Penny came out with Willy on his leash, and he took to sniffing the bushes again.

Some older man came around the house and said hello.

"Are you the campground manager?" I asked.

"Sure, if you want me to be. I own the property and let RVs camp here. It's out of the way of the city and quiet. You staying for the night or longer?" He came closer and looked to be in his eighties. Grey hair and wrinkled like a raisin.

"Just the night. We're on our way to Seattle," I replied.

"Well, that's still a ways away. You can pick any spot you want. As you can see we only have two other RVs parked. The fee is $50 per night. That includes electricity. Just hook up to the extension cord on the ground."

That worried me. I could see it wasn't the best, but it was handy. Penny came up and whispered, "I'm sleeping with my gun."

*

Continued in the book...

~~*~~

Jim Richards Family of Readers

Thanks to the following people who are now part of the Jim Richards Family of Readers. They have read a book or more and enjoyed them. They all volunteered to be included in the list. If you are a fan of the books, send me your full name and you will be included in future books. Send your name to murdernovels@bobmoats.com to be added here and on the website.

* Achim Feifel * Al Norris * Alex Wheatley * Alexandra Delporte-Wilkinson * Amy Tapia * Andrea Bryan * Anne Shepherd * Arianda Sugar * Arlene Markowski * Ashley Augustus * Audra Hall * Barbara Hughes * Barbara Sammons * Barbara Schuler * Barbara Zirger * Beth Donohue Plenskofski * Betsy Childress * Beth Gibson * Bill Sandy * Bill Tornquist * Billie-jo Collie * Boni J Rychener * Carl Bishopric * Carla Lewis * Carole Henderson * Carolyn Conroy * Carolyn Riddle-Linington

* Cassy Bailey * Cathie Turner * Chad Hudson * Charlotte L Duran * Cheryl L. Everett * Cindy Ackley Nunn * Cindy Valstad * Connie Bancroft * Corinne Kay O'Daniel * Dana Robbins Chuchran * Dana Wichita * Danielle Monique * Darren Heald * Dave Travers * David Wilkinson * DeAnn Jannereth * Deanna Miller * Deb Breuker Balbo * Debbie Carter * Debbie White * Deborah Fartuch * Deborah Gauze * Deborah Sullivan * Dee King * Denise Freeman * Diana Carver * Dixie Beck * Donna Gould * Donna Thompson * Donny Minter * Doris Kight * Eddie Moore * Eric Walters * Felicia Annette Bradfield * Francine Menor * Gail Chesney * Georgiann Minster * George Conner * Greg Colucci * Hayley Rankin * Harold Garcia * Heidi Arnold * Irma Ranee Coy * Jacqueline Moss * Jan Kimball * Janice Schneider * Janice Spoor * Jennifer Redmond * Jessica Keown-Belous * Jim Beck * Jo Boguslaw * Jo Turner * Joanne Marie Turner * John Peiffer * John Wisbiski * Joseph Wauro * Joyce Stacy * Joyce Trifiletti * Judy Franklin * Judy Travers * Judy Padgett * Julie Heath * Junnahvee Benson * Karen Dahl * Karen Grams * Karen Higham * Karen Kaiser * Karen Meinburg Richwine * Karen Kirkman Parker * Karin Hawkins * Karin Vasvari * Kathleen Donohue Roesing * Kathleen Riddle-Wolfe * Kathy Hinds Moore * Kathy Jones * Kathy Mitchell * Katie Benzler * Kay Burns * Kelly Garcia * Ken Boggs * Keota Rodriguez * Kiera Mccarthy * Kim Estes * Kitty Stolle * Kristie Sciler * Kirsty Stanton * LaLonnie Scallen * Larry Morris * Leann Parr * Lenora Scales * Leslie Marie Jackson * Linda Forester * Linda Ingle Cox * Linda Kennerö * Linda Magill * Lisa Bower * Liz Gibson * Lorraine Wiman * Loretta Alexander * Lynda Bowles * Lynette Lawrance * LuAnn Louttit * Manny Rothman * Marcia Gibson DeWitt * Marie Calder * Marlene Bryan * MaryLouise Kramp * Mary Lynn Gross * Megan Atkins *

Meghan Hyden * Melody Cannavan * Michael Carruthers * Michael Dinkens * Michael Vannoy * Michelle Burns-Mitchell * Michelle Pilcher * Micki Potter * Mike Moats * Mimi Baur * Myrna Hecht * Nadine Sutton * Nancy Ellen Sayre * Natalie Quine * Neena Martin * O'Della Wilson * Pat Pollington * Pat Rohn * Patricia Jarmon * Patricia C Trezza * Patrick Barry * Paul Lawrance * Peggy Davis * Phyllis Bassett * Raylene Matheny * Rebecca Collins Besner * Renee Brumley * Reta Hanna * Reta Moats * Roberta Navarro-Harder * Sally Berneathy * Sally Hubler * Sarah Santos * Satka Nikc * Sharon E. Edwards * Sharon Mangini * Sharon McMillon * Sheena Rawl * Sherry Amstutz * Shirley Alvarez * Shirley Davies * Shirley Williams * Stacie Rowe * Stephanie Conner * Steve Cullen * Susan Haughton * Susan Hesse Adams * Susan Salomon * Suzan K Chase * Taisha Cullum * Tamara Moore * Tammy Castleberry * Tammy Lynn Wood * Ted Murphy * Terri Atkins * Terri Creech * Terry Raab * Tonia Rachael Riggs-Williams * Travis Fleury-Lopez * Twyla Gawlas * Val Brooks * Walt Munsel * Yvonne Isakson *

Thank you to all these wonderful people.

Thank you for purchasing this book. I hope you enjoy it as much as I enjoyed writing it for my faithful readers. Please feel free to email me to tell me what you thought about my stories. I love hearing from the readers. I can be reached at murdernovels@bobmoats.com thanks again!

www.ingramcontent.com/pod-product-compliance
Lightning Source LLC
Chambersburg PA
CBHW070559130626
46556CB00001B/219
9780692210345